Penciled In

KATRINA AVANT

Katrina'sWORKS
P U B L I S H I N G

ISBN-978-0692480687
ISBN-0692480684

Penciled In
Copyright © June 2015
Katrina Avant
K a t r i n a a v a n t - a u t h o r . c o m

Editor
L.R. Clark

Cover Design
Soul Sister Ink
K a t r i n a s w o r k s . c o m

Dedication

~This book is dedicated to the Most High for all the wisdom, knowledge and courage He has given me. ~

Chapter 1

Myka stared at the text notification that so rudely interrupted her day. The message was from Derrick, her ex. Once again he was trying to draw her into accepting an apology that he didn't mean. Fool me once, she thought. There was no way he was going to get a second chance at manipulating her.

Myka Andria Ellis met Derrick Steele on a singles cruise to the Bahamas sponsored by a local television station. She, along with her girl friends, thought it would be a great way to meet eligible single men. And eligible for them was a man with a great body, handsome face and of course most importantly, a good paying job. Derrick Steele met all of those qualifications along with a few she didn't ask for or want for that matter. Out of the four friends, she and her best friend Cymone were the only ones to come away from the trip with potential mates.

Like Myka, Cymone met what she thought was a good catch, until she learned the man was a habitual gambler. She discovered Jamal, in spite of having a great position with a Fortune 500 corporation, was living with his mother after losing everything in a high stakes poker game. Jamal claimed he was rising above his mistakes and was on a mission to recoup everything he'd lost. Cymone found this ridiculous since he was aiming to regain his wealth at the nearest gambling hall.

With the others, the men on the trip were either too short or too clingy or just plain wrong. Whereas the other two friends may have envied her prize, Myka considered them the lucky ones. She had yet to confide in her girls what Derrick had put her through in just the few months they had been together. In fact, she hadn't gotten around to telling them they were no longer a couple. She didn't know why she was putting it off. It shouldn't have mattered considering she'd had the good sense to get rid of the man for his transgressions. Her girls shouldn't fault her for that.

Myka sighed. They were to meet up at their favorite watering hole after work to get the latest relationship updates, or in her friends Allison and Queen's minds, the dirty. They were dying to know how good Derrick was in bed, but each time one of them brought it up, Myka would gently change the subject. As far as she was concerned, it wasn't any of their business, especially Queen's. The woman seemed to thrive on drama. And her mother always said to watch out for those who were too interested in your love life. They were bound to be after your man. Although Myka didn't think either Allison or Queen fit the bill, she would keep them in the dark just the same.

Aside from keeping their nosiness in check, there was another reason Myka didn't want to talk about her love life with Derrick. The mere thought of them together in bed made her cringe. On top of everything else, the man was a sadist. Derrick would start out caring and gentle, but that would quickly change into something she didn't care for. After his second attempt at drawing her into his painful world, Myka refused to have sex with him. This was yet another reason to want him gone. But the truth was, if Derrick had been the best lover in the world, she would still want him out of her life.

At any rate, she had plenty to tell, but was uncertain as to how much she should reveal to her friends. She didn't want them judging her for allowing Derrick to control her, even if it was for only a short time. She always thought of herself as a smart woman, but with all of Derrick's manipulations and tricks, she felt dumb for accepting his behavior for as long has she had.

Myka was known for her strict scrutiny when it came to men. She never allowed more than a couple of chances for a man to rub her the wrong way. Most of the time the association would end before it really began. She had no tolerance for men who thought they were the prize or for those who wanted to use her for whatever reason. This was what made her relationship with Derrick so embarrassing. Whereas with other men she'd dated, they usually didn't make it past dinner. It perplexed her that she allowed Derrick to remain a full four months, when he should have been booted out the door after the first infraction.

She just couldn't understand why she put up with his egotistical ways as long as she did. Was it because she was lonely and in need of companionship? She had spent the last couple of years seriously growing her business, leaving no room for serious dating. In the beginning, she was doing everything herself, which only left room for a series of dinners or movies that always ended in goodbye. But now that she had employees, she had some spare time on her hands; time that should be spent with someone who cared. She thought Derrick was that someone. She was wrong.

Deleting the message without reading it, Myka turned back to her work as CEO of a small but growing publishing house. Aside from herself, there were two other full time employees: Tessa Andrews, her one and only in-house editor, who doubled as her receptionist; and Mark Cannon, responsible for media and the publishing house's graphic art design department. She also had on hand, a few part-time and called when needed staff members, who mostly worked from home. Everything else her small staff did not handle was left to Myka, and at the moment she was trying to determine if their latest client would be worth the time needed to cultivate him.

When Myka first started Ellis Publications three years ago, she was its sole operator, with dreams of becoming one of the best known in the publishing world. Back then, she published every book that came her way in order to gain the capital she needed to fund Ellis' growth. Now, with twenty authors under her belt, and three of those on the New York Times bestsellers list, she had become more discriminating in the material she accepted. Myka was taking Ellis into a direction that would turn out more bestsellers and not just books. She aimed to find that one author to shoot to that coveted number one spot, which brought her back to her newest submission; a crime drama written by one of Metro City's Assistant District Attorneys, Garrett Pleasant.

A part from viewing the man through sound bites on the local news, Myka had yet to meet him in person. So

far, they had only communicated through email and
Dropbox. While she set appointments to meet face-to-face,
Garrett Pleasant had yet to make any of them due to his
high profile job. Being one of the most sought after
prosecutors in his office, the man was beyond busy. But
that was all supposed to change this afternoon. She had Mr.
Pleasant penciled in for a firm one-on-one meeting to
finally get the ball rolling.

Granted, he had a good story, a great story even, but
Myka wondered if the man himself would sell. She knew
she could take his story to the top, but she questioned if he
could draw the appeal of the readers. Everyone she talked
to seemed to consider him quite dry, aloof even; only
interested in his work to which he claimed to be his only
real focus.

Garrett Pleasant's most recent claim to fame was his
thorough and headline making prosecution of Metro City's
former mayor and police chief. He was instrumental in
taking down the duo's long standing crime ring that
exposed other city officials involved in corruption, human
trafficking, and gun and drug running. He rooted out and
secured the demise of a brutal gang of police officers who
were used as the former mayor's muscle. When Garrett
Pleasant's investigation and prosecution was done, a total

of one hundred and thirteen people were sent to prison, making him the city's crowned hero. If he wasn't knee deep in some criminal case, he was writing about them; hence the new book.

Myka glanced at her watch just as another text buzzed through on her phone. Derrick wanted a response. She guessed he wanted her to forgive him as all the other messages had alluded to. Deleting that message too, she placed the offending phone in a drawer. She needed to prepare for her meeting with Garrett Pleasant without distraction. Glancing at her watch again, she had just over fifteen minutes to decide if she would handle his writing career.

Chapter 2

Garrett Pleasant narrowed his eyes at the man sitting before him. Jason Unger had the nerve to want a plea deal after what he tried to do to his wife and young son—burn them to death.

When his wife Patricia tried leaving their home after he beat her mercilessly, Jason splashed lighter fluid on her and their seven month old son Jamie, and set them on fire. The beating had taken place because she hadn't cooked the potatoes the way he wanted them. Patricia was carrying Jamie as she tried running past her sadistic husband for the front door. She received the majority of the injuries with first and second degree burns covering a large portion of her back and across her shoulders. She shielded young Jamie from most of his father's rage. He only received a few minor burns on the backs of his hands from clinging to his mother's shoulders.

"Mr. Unger, why would you think I would even entertain the idea of a plea for what you've done?" Garrett asked the man in a barely controlled voice. It took everything in him not to leap across the table and beat the shit out of him. He glanced over at the man's attorney who seemed to feel his same sentiments. Although he was there to represent his client, he looked as if he wanted to be anywhere but seated next to the piece of scum.

"If I have my way," Garrett continued. "You will spend a very long time, if not the rest of your life behind bars. Right now, by some miracle, your wife is clinging to life, but if that changes, I will make sure you die at the hands of an executioner."

His wife's injuries weren't nearly as bad as he made them out to be, but Unger didn't know that. Garrett wanted the man scared instead of smirking at him as if he himself held the solution to the world's problems in the palms of his hands. And it worked. Unger's small, self satisfying smile slowly slipped from his face.

Not liking where this was headed, Jason Unger turned to his attorney. "Aren't you going to say something?" he asked the mute man who sat next to him. His attorney, Nate Morrison, took a cleansing breath before answering him.

"Mr. Unger, you didn't exactly leave any wiggle room to negotiate with. You allegedly set your wife and son on fire in a fit of rage. I will do my—."

"You're fired!" Jason screamed at his attorney; pointing at him with handcuffed hands. "You're supposed to be getting me out of this, not help put a needle into my arm. Get out of my face! Get out, both of you! And you better hope like hell I never get out of here or you will pay!" Sneering, his gaze swung from Nate to Garrett.

"Guard!" Garrett called for the guard, before Unger could finish his last sentence. He had better things to do than listen to this despicable man's rant.

When the guard approached him, Unger stood up so abruptly he knocked his metal chair backwards to the floor with a bang; still eyeing both men with contempt as he was led towards the barred door.

Garrett gave Unger a final answering glare before he was hauled from the room still spitting threats.

"Ok, that went well," Nate told his friend and colleague. He and Derrick had gone to college and law school together, and often found themselves in the courtroom as opponents. But thanks to Unger firing him, gratefully not this time.

Still staring after Unger's departure, Nate shook his head. "Man, I'm glad he fired me. I just didn't have it in me to do my best with this case. How is his wife doing? Is she really that bad off?"

Garrett shook his head. "Nah, the doctors say she'll fully recover. I just wanted to get a rise out of the guy. And though I can't make the life thing stick, I still want him to spend a considerable amount of time behind bars for what he did. His wife and child are only alive because he ran out of lighter fluid."

Nate blew out a tense breath. "I take it this isn't his first time abusing them?"

"Nope, not at all. Patricia Unger has endured years of his abuse and each time she got up the nerve to press charges, she would promptly have them dropped and bailed him out of jail. But I think this is the first time he involved the child."

Garrett had seen this too many times to even feel surprised anymore. He was wondering for the umpteenth time, if it was indeed his moment to get out of the game before he became indifferent altogether. After discovering his former co-worker's duplicity concerning the previous mayor's re-election plot and the corruption that rocked the police department, he was more than ready for a change of scenery. This was why he wanted to start a writing career. He could write about the justice system instead of navigating its multifaceted levels of crime and corruption.

"Hey, how did you pull this case anyway?" Garrett asked. "I know for a fact Unger can't afford you."

Nate sighed in frustration. "It was my turn to pull from the ol' pro bono pot and I drew this asshole."

Garrett chuckled. "Well that won't be a problem anymore." Garrett glanced at the clock on the wall. "Shit!" He had forgotten he had an appointment with Ellis Publications and he was twenty minutes late. Grabbing his coat and briefcase, he headed for the door.

"Hey what's the rush, I thought we could do lunch and catch up!" Nate called after him.

"I'll call you later." He hoped he hadn't missed his chance to meet with Ms. Ellis today. This was his third attempt at a meeting and he was sure she wouldn't take too kindly to him showing up late. Each time he was prepared to meet, something always came up.

Pushing his way through the jail's glass doors, he ran the two blocks to the publishing house.

Chapter 3

Tessa Andrews all but licked her lips when she spun around in her chair to the man who cleared his throat to get her attention. She had been off in her own world, trying to recall what she could have done to drive another man from her bed. Her last boyfriend left her without a word. When she went to his job to confront him, she learned, not only had he quit, but had left town to parts unknown. She couldn't understand why he left. She thought they were having a great time together.

Garrett blinked at the woman who was shamelessly sizing him up. "Garrett Pleasant here to see Ms. Ellis," he hesitantly told Tessa with a furrowed brow.

Instantly captivated, Tess let her gaze roam freely over Garrett's body. The man was beyond gorgeous; the type she liked. Her assessment started at his crotch, which was currently at eye level, then worked her way up to his face. Myka told her to expect their newest client today, but after he failed to show at the appointed time, she had crossed out his name in Myka's appointment ledger. Like her boss, she'd only seen the man on television, and from where she was sitting, that flat screen was a liar. She was more than pleasantly surprised at what she saw before her.

Tessa, wearing her receptionist hat at the moment, seductively straightened her back to properly greet their guest, which meant pushing her ample, overexposed breasts front and center.

"Mr. Pleasant, you do realize you're late?" She cooed at him; all the while crossing her legs and swerving suggestively in her chair. Winter cold or not, she was glad she wore her mini skirt today. She made sure he got an eyeful of what could be oh so pleasing. With her last sexual partner quickly forgotten, Tessa grinned at the possibility of having Garrett Pleasant in her bed.

Garrett respectfully eyed the woman as she nearly slid out of the scrap of material that posed as a skirt. Although beautiful, he was never one for the overly aggressive type. He found them to be more trouble than they were worth. He humorously noticed how she made every effort to let him know she was available for whatever he could come up with. But for him, there was absolutely nothing she could do but get him a meeting with her boss.

"Yes I understand. But nevertheless, I was hoping Ms. Ellis could still meet with me, if only for a few minutes. After all, we have been trying to conduct this meeting for awhile now." He gave her his sexiest smile. Two can play this game, he thought. Garrett hoped his efforts would persuade her to pick up the phone to let Myka Ellis know he was standing in her lobby.

But before Tessa could push her breasts forward even more, in an exaggerated reach for the phone, Myka entered the reception area.

"Tessa, I'm going to lunch." She was digging around in her purse for her keys and was unaware they had a guest.

"I will be more than happy to take you to lunch, seeing as I'm late for my appointment."

Myka's head snapped up at the man's deep and intoxicating voice. She felt as if he had caressed her entire body with that one sentence. For a split second she envisioned them naked with her wrapped around his tall muscular frame.

Myka shuddered. *What the hell?*

Pushing the disturbing vision aside, Myka responded. "Mr. Pleasant that's—." She was already set to decline and was poised to turn on her heels to lead him back into her office for their meeting.

Anticipating her hesitation, Garrett quickly added, "Considering my previous cancellations, it's the least that I can do."

He hoped she would say yes for several reasons with the main one giving them the opportunity to get away from the overly sexed receptionist, who was eyeing him as if he were her next tasty meal. There was no doubt in his mind she would make every effort to interrupt their meeting if they stayed in the office. He'd dealt with her type before, and had no desire to spend the time that should be used discussing his book, fending off her advances.

Myka followed Garrett's gaze and glanced over at Tessa. After reading the hunger in the woman's eyes, and the angst in his, she fully understood his desire to vacate the premises.

"Just let me grab my briefcase," she told him. She made a mental note to talk to Tessa later.

Garrett watched Myka walk back towards her office, all the while very aware that Tessa hadn't taken her eyes from him. He glanced at his watch, hoping Myka wouldn't tarry.

"Ready." Myka smiled at the relief that played across Garrett's face. Yes, she would definitely have a nice little talk with Miss Tessa.

***

"May I ask you a question?" Myka asked, once they were seated for lunch.

Garrett shrugged. "Sure."

"Why Ellis Publications?"

He knew what she was asking and the answer was simple. "You are a small publishing house, which means you're hungry and will make every effort to make my book a bestseller. You have something to prove, which means you will give me the most attention; unlike bigger houses who have dozens of clients and twice that many employees. You're local, which for me is important. I can physically meet with you and not be limited to conducting business over the phone or through email. Not to mention, you have an exceptional reputation among your clients. In my opinion, there is no other choice." He ended the accolades with a smile.

"So now, let me ask you a question. What do you think of my manuscript?" He took this time to look over his menu while he awaited her answer.

Myka leaned forward to place her folded hands under her chin. She heard his question, but was at the moment rethinking her concern about Garrett's presence with the readers; especially the female readers. She studied him while he perused his menu and found him more than just attractive. He had an ultra masculine presence that was never conveyed in those thirty second sound bites on the evening news. Garrett Pleasant would definitely wreak havoc on the female literary world without a doubt, and if played just right, every man would want to be him. She knew just how she would sell him. Now was the task of getting him to agree to her plan.

When Myka didn't answer, Garrett peered over the top of his menu to find her studying him as if he were a specimen under glass.

This can't be good.

Unfolding her hands, Myka took a sip from her water glass before she finally answered him. "I think you have a bestseller Mr. Pleasant."

Relieved, he shook his head. "No, please…if we're going to work together you have to call me Garrett."

"Alright Garrett and you may call me Myka." Placing her hands into her lap, she gave him a small smile before continuing. "And as I was saying, your work is bestseller material. And I hope you don't take this the wrong way, but…we need to do a bit of work on your persona.

Garrett's glass stopped in mid air, as he was about to take a drink from his tea. "My persona?"

"Don't get me wrong, you are an attractive man; tall, dark and handsome, along with everything else women like. And I am sure you can attest to this due to my receptionist's response to you. But what I have in mind is changing a few things to make you bigger than life. Even though your book is a crime drama, I want to make it sexy as well. Can you add a few steamy love encounters between the hero and one or more of the female characters?" Myka held up her hand to stop him from speaking. The way he opened his mouth and narrowed his eyes, said he had objections, but she wanted him to hear her out first.

"And we need to loosen you up a bit." She took in his attire which was perfect for the courtroom, but not so much for the reading public. Plus, she had no doubt in her mind that his off the clock attire didn't venture far from what she was viewing at the moment.

Garrett frowned. He didn't want his book to become some sort of a romance novel; just the facts—thank you ma'am—and nothing more. But it looked as if his future publisher had some other things in mind as well.

Putting his concerns for the book aside, he wondered about her suggestion in changing his character. "What do you mean loosen me up?"

"Let me ask you this. What do you wear when you're not at the office?"

He shrugged. "A pair of slacks and your run of the mill button down shirt." He saw nothing wrong with his choice of dress, until he caught her frown.

Myka rolled her eyes. She knew it. "There lies the problem. You are a young, successful, good looking man who should present himself accordingly. Your choice of style suggests boring. And if we don't loosen your grip on that, the readers won't buy into the picture you're trying to paint with your story, no matter how great a book you have.

Garrett turned over what she said. He never saw himself as dull before today. Looking down at his clothing, he quickly glanced around at the other men who were in the restaurant; taking close notice of those about his age. There was a smattering of sports attire; some jeans and button downs; a couple of long sleeve tees with sneakers or Timberlands. Aside from a couple of elderly gents, He seemed to be the only one wearing business attire. And although his business dress consisted of suits, Garrett spent quite a bit of money to ensure they fit him with precision. He was no slouch when it came to dressing appropriately.

But he asked himself, if it were Saturday afternoon, would he fit in with the other men? He had to concede that the answer was a resounding no.

With a resigned sigh, he reluctantly asked her opinion. "So what do you suggest?" He hoped she didn't want him to dress like some rap star donning oversized, low riding pants, sporting gold chains around his neck.

Sitting forward, Myka gleefully rubbed her hands together. "Now we're talking." She held up a finger of caution at his unenthusiastic frown. "Nothing major…just a slight wardrobe adjustment that's all. And maybe a slight attitude adjustment." She laughed at the indignant look he gave her.

After ordering their meals, Myka pulled her iPad from her briefcase. While she searched for whatever she was looking for, Garrett took his turn to study her.

Myka Ellis' talk of attractiveness certainly included her. She was fit, shapely and beautiful in every sense of the word. Unlike Tessa, Myka didn't appear to be aware of how beautiful she was. He could tell by the way she kept patting at her hair and straightening her clothes, as if she were dissatisfied with herself. It didn't seem to matter that she was dressed to the nines in clothing that fit and suited her well. Her attire only enhanced her natural beauty, revealing everything sexy about her without being inappropriate.

The blouse she wore had just a hint of cleavage to warrant a glance, but not enough to cause a stare the way Tessa's had. Myka's skirt, although above her knees, was by no means nearly as short as Tessa's either. Not one time did it ride up, no matter how much she moved around on her chair. In his opinion, she had no worries. Myka Ellis was perfect. He liked everything he saw. And from the looks of some of the other men in the room, they did too. More than once he caught a few of them stealing glances in their direction.

"Here", she handed him the tablet, pointing out a male model in a magazine advertisement.

Although the man was wearing a casual pair of cotton slacks, the difference between them stopped there. Whereas he would sport a blue or black loose pullover or shirt, the model wore a more vibrant colored shirt with the clinging fabric defining every bulging muscle; the shirt's sleeves were pushed slightly above the wrists with the shirt tails free. He frowned at this. He was never one to wear a shirt unless the tails were tucked in and neatly secured by a belt.

Redirecting his gaze, Garrett viewed the fit of the shirt again. He unconsciously flexed his own biceps and pecs. He preferred room in his shirts rather than the fitted attire the man was wearing. Scrutinizing the overall attire, he felt there was room for compromise on his part.

Garrett tapped the screen to enlarge the photo; zooming in on the watch the man wore. He had one like it, so no problem there. He moved from his wrist down to the model's feet; closing in on the fairly expensive shoes. The soft handmade loafers were something he could pull off too. He shrugged. If this was all she had in mind, he could live with it.

Myka grinned. Garrett didn't balk at the style she was suggesting. He seemed to be onboard with that aspect of change.

"Now let's talk about your demeanor."

Chapter 4

Garrett sat in his office recalling his lunch with Myka Ellis. It was interesting to say the least. By the time they were finished with their meal, she had his head spinning. Who knew there was such a production outside of writing a book to make it sell? It was more work than he bargained for.

He shook his head. Although he initially scoffed at her suggestions of putting some fire into his novel, after she read some of the more drier portions of the book, he had to admit, it did need some help. But the trick was, what should he place there and how much? He didn't know where to begin.

Garrett dated sparingly, and when he did find the time to entertain a woman, he had to admit, he never took the time to inject passion or sex appeal into the encounters. He spent most of his early adult life preparing for his career as an attorney. And after passing the bar, it was internship and now the district attorney's office. His idea of a relationship only averaged a few weeks at most, with his work load usually driving women away. So his approach to sex was simple: let's just get it done. But now, after listening to Myka Ellis' suggestions, he realized he knew very little about what it took to deliberately seduce a woman.

Contemplating his dilemma, Garrett rubbed long manicured fingers across his closely shaven chin. Where *did* he begin? His body knew where he should start, because it had already begun without him. While he sat across from Myka, as she talked of ways to spice up his book, he was thinking of ways to get her underneath him in bed.

Garrett never had to be aggressive when it came to women; they always made themselves available without any effort on his part. But in Myka's case, he wanted to make an exception. Whereas most women flocked to him without effort, she kept everything on a business level, never wavering from it once. He was attracted to her the moment she stepped into the lobby of her office. He knew he would have to work at convincing her to spend time with him for reasons other than business, but he had already cleared the first hurdle in swaying her, by getting her to agree to lunch. He could thank Myka's receptionist for that inspiration.

Grabbing up the phone, he had an idea on how he could accomplish more from her.

*****

Myka reached for the phone to ask Tessa to step into her office. She was away from her desk when she returned from lunch, but she now heard her stilettos click-clacking on the tiled floor, as she passed her door on the way to her desk.

It bothered her how the woman threw herself at Garrett. He was a client and should have been treated as such. Tessa had always been a little obsessive and pushy when it came to men. Up until now, she kept her nonsense outside of the office. Myka ran a respectable business and losing clients, because of an over-heated employee, was not an option. She was just grateful Garrett was a good sport about it all. He never once complained of Tessa's actions during lunch, although she had expected him to. Tessa was way out of line.

But before she could buzz the young woman to join her in her office, Tessa notified her she had a call. It was Garrett. Myka cringed before lifting the receiver. She dared to wonder what nasty things Tessa said to the man before handing the call off to her. She would talk with her immediately after speaking with him.

"Garrett, I didn't expect to hear from you so soon. But since you're calling, I'm guessing you've thought over my suggestions." She hoped that was all he had to comment on. Myka held her breath while she awaited his answer. She didn't have to worry. Garrett had easily deflected Tessa's advances.

"Yes I have, and I realized that you're right. I do need to make a few changes in my book as well as with my public persona. And that's why I called. I need you to help me in both areas, starting with my attire. I'm leaving work early this evening and I was hoping you would join me on a little shopping spree, seeing as you have all the ideas on how I should look." Garrett smiled as he anticipated her answer. He knew this was the last thing she expected and her next question proved it.

"Well, um…you don't have a girlfriend or sister to help you make those decisions?" When she suggested wardrobe changes she didn't mean she should participate in making that happen. Even though she was good at dressing men, her ex Derrick could attest to that, she had no intentions of helping Garrett with his clothing choices. Especially after that vision she had of them earlier. That was all she needed, to accidently see him half undressed or God forbid completely naked.

As she searched her mind for an excuse not to accompany him, Garrett pushed forward. "Unfortunately I am an only child, so there is no sister and no I don't have a girlfriend. Right now my job is too demanding to be in a relationship. So I guess you're it. That is, if you're serious about me making these changes you proposed."

Garrett knew he had her then. Myka Ellis was a perfectionist and anything she deemed worthy she would make sure it happened. And he was guessing this was no different. He knew if she wanted his personality upgraded she would have to do it herself or take a chance on him going at it alone and making a mess of it. And failure for her was not an option.

Myka realized she really didn't have a choice. Looking over her evening schedule, she didn't have anything pressing that would prevent her from clothes shopping with him. And she did want this done right.

Finally relenting, she agreed. He promised to meet her at her office within the hour. But before placing the receiver back onto its cradle, Myka pressed the intercom to summon Tessa into her office. It was time to put the woman in her place before Garrett arrived for the second time that day. She did not want Tessa's earlier games repeated.

Chapter 5

If Myka acted more like me, she'll get laid more than once a decade.

Tessa Andrews sat at her desk fuming. She had just left Myka's office where she received what she considered an unfair tongue lashing. She couldn't believe the woman had the nerve to tell her she was acting like a bitch in heat.

In her opinion, Myka had always been a stuck up bitch; always playing too good for the likes of her. Oh, she was pleasant enough, but Tessa could see it in her eyes that she didn't care much for her. She couldn't understand why she was so upset about her coming on to Garrett Pleasant. The man was single and available to any woman who wanted him, and that included her. Just because Myka didn't want him didn't mean she had the right to keep her away from him.

Tapping her desk in frustration with red acrylic nails, Tessa's face softened when her eyes landed on her computer screen. It was okay. She had Garrett's information, so she would just use it to conveniently drop here and there to get the man's attention. She didn't think it would take much for her to sway him, considering the way his eyes followed her skirt as it rode up her thighs. And he did playfully taunt her when he called earlier. Tessa's pleased smile lifted her sour mood. Garrett liked what he saw and if Myka hadn't come out of her office when she had, she and Garrett would be spending the night in his bed. She was sure of it.

With renewed vigor, Tessa pulled up Garrett's home and work information. Jotting down what she needed, she placed the slip of paper into her purse. There was always more than one way to get what you wanted. And she wanted Garrett Pleasant.

Satisfied, Tessa ran her perfectly manicured fingers through her equally perfect precision cut blonde hair. She may have found a way around Myka, but she was still put off by the woman's audacity. She would pay the bitch back somehow. She had no right to interfere in her personal life, no right at all.

While Tessa searched her mind for a just retaliation, the phone rang. She smiled at the caller displayed. She realized this was just what she needed.

***

Chapter 6

After recognizing the voice on the other end of the phone, Myka closed her eyes with mildly contained contempt. It was Derrick.

She could just kill Tessa. She was not, under any circumstances, to allow his calls through, but here she was, sharing a conversation with a man she had grown to loath. Frowning, Myka knew all too well why she was having this exchange. This was Tessa's payback for setting her straight on flirting with clients, namely Garrett Pleasant. It would do no good to chastise her. The catty woman would only claim ignorance. Myka ground her teeth while she listened to her ill chosen love interest speak.

"Myka, I know I may have been a little over the top with some of the things I've done," Derrick was saying; bringing her unwillingly back to the conversation. "And I am willing to admit I was wrong and will make every effort to correct my mistakes. Baby I miss you, and I know you miss me, even if you won't admit it. Just give us another try, huh? Just think about it and I will give you a call later in the week and we'll have lunch to discuss things."

"Derrick wait!" Myka shouted into the phone, but he had ended the call. She wanted to throw something, anything. "What part of I want you out of my life do you not understand?" she asked the dead phone through clenched teeth. "Ughhhh!"

Slamming down the receiver, she sprang from her chair. She was headed straight for Tessa, but quickly stopped herself. She wouldn't give that cow the satisfaction of knowing she was upset. She couldn't let her rattle her nerves like that.

Dropping back into her chair, Myka blew out a long, frustrated and angry breath. She wished she'd never met Derrick Steele. This is why she didn't date, and after dealing with him, she vowed it would be the last relationship she would be a part of. She placed her head on her desk as she thought over what made Derrick so distasteful. When she first met him, he appeared to be everything she could ever want in a man, but it had only taken a few months to prove that theory wrong. He turned out to be the worst man she had ever encountered.

***

Myka met Derrick on the second day of a five day cruise around the Caribbean. She and her friends had left the ship to explore St. Lucia, a beautiful island that she hoped to visit again someday. The travel agency had timed their trip to coincide with the islands annual jazz festival and they were in attendance. Drink in hand and swaying to the wonderful music, Myka was having a wonderful time with her friends when Derrick approached her. He was pleasant enough, and traveling alone, so she invited him to join their merry band of revelers.

For the rest of the trip, she and Derrick found time to pair off to get to know one another. She would spend the better part of the days with the girls, but the evenings were for dining with Derrick, which she found intriguing. She liked him and after discovering they lived in the same city, promised to keep in touch once they were home.

At first, everything was wonderful. He was attractive, fun and attentive, but that soon changed. The changes started off small; barely noticeable. The first thing to catch her attention was his planning things for them to do, only to change the venue or time at the last moment without explanation. She was usually told of the change of plans, only after they were in the car and on their way. It could be something as simple as asking her where she wanted to go for lunch, only to take her someplace else. Or suggesting they have a night out on the town, only to have his mother waiting in the car when she climbed inside; usually with her sitting in the back seat, since Mrs. Steele refused to sit anywhere but next to her son. She called this behavior Derrick's bait and switch or in other words, Derrick's deceptive character.

There were times he would tell her he was one place only to be somewhere else. Once, after not hearing from him in over a week, he showed up in photos on Facebook at some party that he claimed was no big deal. But if it was no big deal, then why didn't she know about it and why wasn't she invited?

Well it was a big deal, considering the woman who hosted the party—according to Derrick—wanted him in her bed in the worst way. The woman wanted him enough that she contacted Myka to inform her of the true nature of their relationship; which meant Derrick had lied about his involvement with the woman from the start. The woman knew too many details about Myka's relationship to Derrick for him not to have confided in her. The woman even went on to claim she didn't have a problem sharing Derrick, if they both were woman enough to handle such a thing.

When she told Derrick of the woman's call, he made light of it; stating she only made those accusations to get under her skin. Myka may have over looked her as a woman wanting to start trouble, had it not been for the other things *and* the other women; women he claimed he only humored to get what he wanted or needed from them at the time. His flippancy about the whole matter was what bothered her the most. Derrick was so comfortable with his deceptive lifestyle that he saw nothing wrong with making such a confession. Myka realized then she was just a placeholder in his life; just something to do, like all the other women he claimed meant nothing—unless he was using them.

Myka had always prided herself in being an intelligent woman, but with Derrick, she had made stupid mistakes. And the biggest of them all was sleeping with him. He had her believing she was the only woman for him and that they were going to build a life together. He even went so far as to buy a ring. But when he tried placing it on her finger it was too small. He supposedly took it to be resized only she never saw it again. And when she asked him about it, he would wave it off, claiming it was still being serviced and then he would quickly change the subject.

That's when she knew for certain she meant nothing to him. He had no intentions of marrying her. The performance with the proposal and the ring was to keep her hopeful, until he was finished playing with her. She bet he saw her on that cruise and set his plans for her then. Myka felt this was Derrick Steele's true persona; this was how he operated. Women were just a means to an end for him, nothing more. And unfortunately she happened to be in that number.

Derrick had penciled her into his life for whatever role she was to play at the time, only to be erased away without a moment's notice. She and the other women were all pawns in his cat and mouse game of manipulation and mental abuse. Derrick was used to being the one to end a relationship or in her case, some sick partnership where he reaped all the benefits. And she knew the only reason he was gung-ho in getting her back under his thumb, was to break her for having the audacity to leave him. The decision to walk away was never supposed to be left up to the prey.

Myka sat up. She could kick herself for not seeing him sooner. She never wanted to sleep with another man that didn't love her and didn't have her best interests at heart. It made her sick to think how she fell for Derrick Steele. The mere thought of that colossal blunder made her cry. She had worked so hard to establish herself as a woman who knew what she wanted; one who didn't take any foolishness as a compromise. But there she was, taken in by a man she should never have allowed into her life at any level. In this aspect, she was a failure and a fraud, and it shamed her.

The phone buzzed, releasing her from her self-loathing. Myka wiped away the tears that had settled on her cheeks and answered Tessa's page. Garrett was waiting for her.

Retrieving her compact from her purse, she repaired her face and moist eyes. When she was satisfied that no one would suspect she had been crying, she replaced everything, grabbed her things and headed for the lobby.

Plastering on an award winning smile, Myka stepped into the reception area. She would have a great evening of shopping and remaking Garrett Pleasant. Spending time doing one of the things she loved, would take her mind off of her troubles with Derrick Steele.

Chapter 7

Garrett watched Tessa type away on her keyboard.
She had done a complete turnaround from his earlier visit.
He fully expected the woman to be all over him once he
cleared the door, but she just greeted him, and asked him to
have a seat while she let Myka know he had arrived. There
were no hints of the implied suggestions she made when he
called; no coy looks or unspoken innuendos, and he was
relieved. Garrett assumed Myka was responsible for the
woman's change and he was more than grateful. He was on
a mission, and battling Myka's receptionist was not part of
the plan.

He had only waited a few minutes before Myka
emerged from her office. Though she smiled, he studied
her. Something was off in her appearance. The smile
displayed on her lips didn't reach her eyes. He had been a
prosecutor long enough to recognize discomfort when he
saw it. He continued to watch her as she walked towards
him. She didn't glance towards Tessa and Tessa never
looked up from her monitor. His guess was correct. The
two had words. And from both women's avoidance of the
other, evidently they weren't comfortably given or
received.

Myka spoke when she reached him. "You know, I fully expected you to be late or call to cancel," Myka told him. "I didn't even bother to write you into my appointment book this time." She couldn't help teasing him. Although she was reluctant earlier, she was glad he was there. After the afternoon she'd had, she needed a distraction, and shopping always helped to soothe her nerves.

With his hands in his pockets, Garrett rocked on his heels. He had to concede he had that coming. But he would make it a point to never be late or stand her up again. He had a new mission, and it involved getting *Myka Ellis* to loosen up and have some fun. He had a few things planned, and if all went well, at some point in the future, those plans would end with Myka as a long term fixture in his life.

Garrett shook his head. "I am going to make every effort to make sure that never happens again. So are you ready for some fun?"

Garrett offered her his arm which she gladly grasped. He led her through the glass doors down to the bank of elevators, while a frowning Tessa looked on.

"Well good for her."

Tessa jumped at the sudden voice in the quiet room. It was the end of the day and she thought everyone else had gone by now. But Mark Cannon was still there, leaning against a wall with his arms folded.

"What are you talking about?" Tessa asked him in a huff.

She loathed Mark. When she first arrived there, she tried turning her charms on him, only to have him call her on it. Mark hated the way she carried herself and told her so. He told her she needed to clean up her act because she was one step away from becoming a full-fledged tramp. He didn't like her attitude and the feeling was mutual.

"Myka. It's about time she met someone who was worthy of her. That ass Derrick didn't know what to do with a woman like Myka, but Mr. Garrett Pleasant, I like. He's a genuine gentleman and he knows how to treat a lady. Something I'm sure you know nothing about," Mark quipped.

He couldn't resist sticking it to Tessa. He had the displeasure of witnessing her whorish display earlier and almost applauded when the man didn't take the bait. The trouble with Tessa, she thought every man wanted her. He almost felt sorry for her—almost.

"That man doesn't want her. She's too slow for him." She couldn't believe he would even suggest such a thing. "Besides, Myka will have her hands full dealing with Derrick." The corners of Tessa's mouth crept upward.

Mark's eyes narrowed. "What the hell did you do?"

Tessa said nothing. She grabbed her purse from her desk drawer, donned her coat and swept past him towards the elevators. Myka Ellis would not be a problem for her when she finally snared Garrett; she made certain of that.

***

Derrick Steele smiled with his hands placed behind his head. He rocked with renewed confidence in his expensive, butter soft leather chair. Everything in his office was expensive, from the carpet, to the paintings that graced the walls. And he could afford every object and then some.

Two years ago he made partner with one of the most prestigious law firms in the country. Along with the earned partnership, came the trappings of wealth that pumped up his already delusional right to self-importance. Something he felt he more than deserved. Unlike some of his law school acquaintances, he hadn't had wealth handed to him on a silver platter. Anything he wanted he had to take and what he wanted at the moment was retribution against Myka Ellis.

He knew she was just playing coy and it was confirmed when Tessa let him in on Myka's secret. She still wanted him and he just needed to be more persistent in getting her back. He would have to be gentler with her and more 'loving' to win her back into the fold. Well, if persistence and the illusion of love was what it took, then she needed to get ready. He was going to pull out all the stops.

Derrick wanted Myka the moment he saw her step from a cab downtown. He hadn't known who she was or where to find her, until he saw Tessa talking to her one morning in the coffee shop. After discovering she was Tessa's boss, everything else had been easy.

Tessa let it slip that Myka and some friends were taking a cruise. He immediately booked his cabin and set his trap. He shook his head. He had to leave the country in order to meet a woman who lived right there in the city. But once he'd met her, he schemed to keep her for as long as she interested him.

Myka was perfect. She was intelligent, driven and sophisticated, unlike most of the women he met. Sure he had met some gorgeous and wonderful women, but those he met were usually like him; they had an agenda. Namely, they all wanted him for his money and prestige. And he would oblige them until he tired of them, which didn't take long. But Myka was different. She didn't want anything from him and that was the attraction. There was just something about Myka that clicked for him.

Derrick frowned. If it hadn't been for his mother, he would still have Myka under his control. Janice Steele demanded everything from her only son. That meant money, her lifestyle and most of all, his time. His mother had always been domineering, even before his father died. Most of the time Janice's demands didn't bother him. All he had to do was give her another credit card or sponsor another one of those trips she liked to take. But when she meddled into his personal life that was unacceptable. When the time came, he would make sure she was paid back in full for disrupting his time with Myka.

He allowed his mother to control many things in his life, but when he should dump a woman was not one of them. Janice had put one of Derrick's playmates up to calling Myka with some of their more intimate details, driving Myka away from him. For Derrick, Myka's luster had started to fade and if Janice had kept out of his business, she would have been gone soon enough. But Myka's premature exit had cost him the high of letting her free fall into emotional ruin. For him, that scenario never got old. He enjoyed breaking women down. It was almost as good a high, as winning a difficult court case.

Derrick grinned knowingly. His mother was so busy trying to control his life that she missed the one thing that was right there under her nose. There would come a day when he would gladly enlighten her, but now wasn't the time. His grin widened. When he did reveal his secret, it would put a guaranteed end to their family ties once and for all. But in the meantime, he had his reconciliation with Myka to prepare for.

He would start his campaign in winning her back this weekend. He planned to bombard her with her every heart's desire. He made a list of everything she'd mentioned that she loved or wanted, and he was going to make sure she had everything on that list over the next few weeks. By the time he finished wooing her, she would fall at his feet with gratitude.

Derrick smirked. And that's when he would crush her.

Chapter 8

Cymone downed her drink after ordering another from the passing server. She'd had a rough day and was happy to end it with alcohol. Looking over her shoulder, she locked eyes with the man who had been staring at her since the moment she arrived. But with the way she was feeling, he could have been the king of Siam and she wouldn't have care. She'd had enough of men for awhile. After the fiasco with Jamal, she was more than ready for a break. Rolling her eyes, she turned away from the staring man.

"Gurl…where the hell is Myka? She was 'posed to be here an hour ago."

Not only was the word 'supposed' mangled, but 'here' came out as 'err', further irritating Cymone. This was from Queen; Cymone's least favorite person of their group.

Cymone disliked everything about Queen, from her claw-like acrylic nails, to her kitchen whipped, spiked, blonde hair. And tonight, she had the nerve to sport lavender contact lenses. She couldn't understand why a parent would give such a name to a woman who was anything but a queen. Not to mention, whenever the woman opened her mouth, she sounded like an extra from some ghetto sitcom.

Cymone rolled her eyes again and sighed. She wished Myka would hurry up so she wouldn't have to endure Queen Bitch in all of her ghetto glory. Queen was Myka's friend who she felt the need to include in all of their get-togethers. Whenever they were all together, Myka would play referee between her and Queen. She knew how much Cymone disliked her. Spending anytime with the woman was something she abhorred.

"Myka had a last minute client meeting, so she won't be joining us tonight," Allison told her. She was equally disappointed that Myka couldn't make it. Not because she disliked Queen, but she wanted to hear all about Derrick. Allison didn't like the fact that Myka had been keeping everything about the man so close to the vest. But she could understand why, considering how fine the man was. If Derrick were hers, she wouldn't give other women the low-down either. She just wished she had met him before Myka had gotten her claws in him. In Allison's opinion, Myka and Cymone always hooked up with the best men.

Cymone ignored both women and downed her second drink before the server could place it on the table. If Myka wasn't coming she was leaving.

"Look ladies, I'm out." She pulled some money from her purse and handed the wad to Allison. "Pay the woman when she comes back," she told her. She didn't feel like entertaining Heckle and Jeckle tonight. She liked Allison well enough; she just didn't want to be bothered. Cymone grabbed her coat and headed for the door.

"Hey!" Queen whined. She didn't want her to leave. It wasn't fun unless all of them were together. Even though Myka couldn't make their little party, she had hoped the three of them could still have a good time.

Allison waved a hand at Cymone's retreating back. "Girl let her go. She's had her panties twisted since she got here." She didn't care if she left. The person she wanted to see was Myka anyway.

"Oooo gurl, look at those guys over there. They are some kinda fine. I wonder if they would mind a little company. Come on Allison, let's go introduce ourselves." Queen was out of her chair before Allison could respond.

"Nah, you go ahead. I'll just wait here." Allison wasn't in the mood to put on a show for a bunch of horny guys tonight. There was only one man for her and that was

Derrick Steele. She hoped against hope that Myka would find something wrong with the man and toss him aside. She would gladly be there to pick him up.

Queen shrugged. "Suit yourself." Smoothing her dress along her generous hips, she sashayed across the crowded bar towards the group of men.

Allison watched her work awhile, before pulling her phone from her purse. Dialing Myka's number she got her voicemail. Disappointed, she shoved the phone back in her over crowded bag and pouted. She really wanted to know what was going on with her and Derrick.

***

Cymone waited in front of the valet stand for her car. She clutched her cashmere coat tighter to keep the wind from chilling her body.

"I was hoping to buy you a drink." A man's voice suddenly materialized at her side.

Startled, Cymone nearly jumped out of her skin. It was her stalker from the bar. She was so deep in thought she hadn't heard the man walk up.

Putting some distance between them, Cymone cocked her head to the side to stare up at him. He had to be at least six-three to her petite five-foot four frame. As she studied his face, she felt she knew him from somewhere before tonight. She just couldn't place where. He was handsome; nicely dressed. His smile displayed the fact that he had all of his teeth, which were as white as chalk. They complimented his mocha skin nicely. But she wasn't interested and was about to tell him so when he spoke again.

"Before you say no to dinner, here is my card. Just think about it and give me a call when you've decided I'm not a bad guy." He nodded at her before turning on his heels to re-enter the bar.

Cymone glanced down at the card. "Nathaniel Morrison, Attorney at Law." Cymone raised her brow. She noted the name of the law firm, Bennett Law Group, PLLC. Maybe that's where she knew him from. A television commercial perhaps? This firm was always on television for something or other.

She rubbed a finger across the card. Not too shabby. Top quality paper with expensive lettering. And with the way he was dressed, she assumed he was very successful at his craft. Cymone placed the card in her purse just as the valet brought her car around. She wasn't interested, but would keep the card just the same.

Chapter 9

Before removing her shoes, Myka tossed her purse and coat onto a nearby chair.

What a night. Not only had she helped in building a totally new wardrobe for Garrett, he insisted that he take her to dinner to thank her. She had hoped to join the girls for their planned outing and tried begging off, but he wouldn't hear of her leaving without feeding her. And feed her he did.

The man found one of the most expensive restaurants in the area to thank her. She had wanted to try the food there, but the entrees were a little out of her price range. She may have dressed in designer duds, but she was far from rich. Myka saw her designer pieces as investments into her future. If she was going to grow her company, she needed to be taken seriously and her wardrobe screamed she meant business.

Opening the cupboard for a wine goblet, she poured herself a healthy glass and took it to her sofa. Taking a sip, she let the white wine warm her soul. She thought about her time with Garrett. It was nice—no it was better than nice, it was fun. Once they arrived at the second store, he was more than into the shopping. Swaggering from the dressing room and spinning like Ne-Yo in one of his videos. All Garrett needed was some background music.

Myka smiled at the memory. She hadn't realized how much Garrett looked like the man he unwittingly tried to portray, until he made that little move. Garrett Pleasant had a little soul in him after all. Her smile widened at the thought of the man himself. He wasn't as stuffy as she initially thought. At least he kept an open mind about her suggestions. There was more to him than met the eye; more than she suspected he even knew. He'd mentioned at dinner that he hadn't relaxed like that in years. She believed him. When he relaxed, the true Garrett shined through. He wasn't in prosecutor mode, something he himself didn't think he could break free of, but tonight he had.

Myka's smile faltered a little when she recalled another topic of conversation they had during dinner. Tessa. Garrett brought her up without mentioning how unprofessional she was, although that was just how Tessa betrayed herself. Myka was a little embarrassed over her actions and told him so. He waved it off, stating that he didn't blame her. He knew the type, and if the moment ever repeated itself, he would handle it. But Myka assured him he wouldn't have to, because she had taken care of it.

Myka's smile returned. Garrett may have been hardcore in the courtroom, but he was more down to earth than she expected. Garrett was nothing like Derrick. In fact, he was the complete opposite. Garrett's personality shined through as someone who was sincere, genuine. He had all of the characteristics that never showed up in Derrick not even from the beginning. Yes, there was more to Garrett Pleasant, and against her better judgment, she wanted to get to know that part he didn't show the public.

"What am I thinking? The man is a client." Myka rose from her seat to head for her bedroom to prepare for bed.

Chapter 10

Nate watched Cymone drive away before settling himself at his place at the bar for another beer. There was no way he was going to let her leave without saying something to her. He spotted her the moment she arrived. Time seemed to stand still while she glanced around the crowded space looking for her party. She stood out among the other women in the bar, who were eyeing every man in the place as a potential husband. She stood out because she appeared not to want anything from anyone.

He noticed the scowl that played across her face after spotting someone towards the back of the room. Nate understood immediately upon noticing the two women who were waving her over. They were not in her league. Where she was classy and subdued, they were loud and obnoxious, one more than the other. With the way she eyed them, he wondered if they were even friendly. Especially with the one who was now rubbing her groove thang up against the crotch of the man she was dancing with.

Nate shook his head. He turned his attention to the other woman. Although she seemed to be a bit more restrained than her friend, there was still something off about her. He just couldn't put his finger on it. He turned and reached for his beer, just as someone clasped him on the back. It was Garrett.

"Hey old man, why are you sitting here alone tonight? I thought you would have snagged at least one of these women by now." Garrett settled himself on the next stool and raised a finger to get the bartenders attention for a beer of his own.

Nate, taking a swallow from his, shook his head. "Nah, I'll leave the snagging to you partner. Say, you flew out of the jail this afternoon like you were on fire. What gives?"

He took a sip from the glass the bartender put before him. "I had a pressing appointment."

Garrett didn't know how much he should tell his old friend, so he kept the details to himself. He wasn't ready just yet to reveal his future career move. Everyone would think he was nuts if he told them he wanted to quit the D.A.'s office to become a writer, especially since the timing was considered at the height of his career. And after the city's top level corruption convictions, he was more sought after than ever before. But that was just what he wanted to do. And even if he failed, he had enough money to take him well into the next life, thanks to his parents, who provided him with a healthy trust fund if he needed it.

Garrett grew up surrounded by love as well as wealth. But his parents made sure the money didn't spoil him, especially his father. Even though he didn't have to, his dad worked just as hard as any man who didn't have two nickels to rub together. Mason Pleasant made sure his son knew the value of a dollar. Not many people knew how rich he was, which left most wondering how he managed to afford expensive clothes and an expensive car on a civil servants salary. Nate was one of the few people who knew, along with Derrick Steele, with whom they both attended law school.

But now, he had little to do with Derrick and avoided the man as much as possible. But that wasn't always the case. At one time, Garrett considered Derrick one of his closest friends, sharing everything. That was until Derrick took the sharing a little too far. He, Nate and Derrick used to be like brothers before Derrick forced him and Nate to make a choice in their friendship.

Now, whenever they bumped into each other in the courthouse, they never actually speak. They awkwardly acknowledge one another with a nod. Nate, even though he didn't agree with Derricks tactics, still had drinks with him from time to time. Nate's philosophy was to keep your enemies very close. Garrett, on the other hand, was just grateful Derrick specialized in corporate law instead of criminal, which lessened the chances of them crossing paths.

Nate chuckled. "Oh, so you're just going to keep the nature of your business to yourself?" He knew his friend would tell him in his own time. That was just how Garrett operated when it came to personal matters. And after that debacle with Derrick, he understood why.

Garrett grinned back. "I will tell you this. I met the most interesting woman." He was still thinking about Myka. He was glad she accepted dinner with him.

"Oh yeah? Who is she?" Nate turned to give him his full attention. He had been watching the dancing queen's friend size up Garrett. Yep, he had those two pegged right for sure.

"I mean, you never talk about women. Ever. Come to think of it, when have you had time for women?" He couldn't remember the last time Garrett had been on a date, so this should be interesting.

Catching movement out of the corner of his eye, Nate's attention was drawn back to the woman eyeing Garrett. She was headed their way.

Garrett drank some more of his beer. "Her name is Myka Ellis," he told him. "And I had dinner with her tonight.

He raised an eyebrow, at not just what Garrett said, but at the woman who planted herself next to him listening. The woman inched closer while she pretended to be after a drink from the bartender. She was just about to say something, when Garrett mentioned his date's name. The woman's mouth flew open in shock, as if she knew who he was talking about.

"Really? I've heard of her. And from what I hear, she's an up and coming force to be reckoned with in the publishing world. And if my memory serves me correctly, I also hear she's a looker." Nate said this to Garrett, but was still eyeing the woman. She had yet to notice he was watching her. She was too focused on what Garrett was saying to pay him any attention

"Yes she is on all counts. We had a very interesting evening and I plan to see more of her."

"So I take it the lady is unattached?" Nate asked; scrutinizing the nosy woman for a reaction.

Swallowing a mouthful of beer, Garrett nodded. "Yes she is. She's recently become available, so it's a go on my part. I just have to convince her that I'm worthy of her time." And he would prove it to her one day at a time.

Nate watched the eavesdropper turn on her heels; nearly running in the direction of her friend. But not before he caught the devious little smile that played across her lips. This woman definitely knew Ms. Ellis and was about to make trouble for either her, Garrett or both of them. He hoped like hell the woman he gave his card to called him. He needed to find out what was going on and stop this one in her tracks.

***

"Girl, you are *not* going to believe what I just heard," Allison told Queen, after pulling her away from the guy she was dancing with. She knew Queen was mad, but would soon get over it when she heard what she had to spill.

"Hey! I was into that guy," Queen whined. She turned to blow kisses at her dance partner, who could have cared less, since he had pulled another woman's backside against his growing groin. He didn't even look her way. Queen huffed with disgust, turning her attention back to Allison.

"Ok gurl, spill it."

"I overheard that guy over there…the one who looks like Ne-Yo, mention Myka and how she was unattached. He was telling his friend how he plans to get to know her better. Girl, Myka and Derrick aren't together anymore." Allison was about to jump out of her chair with glee. The way had been paved for her to be with Derrick.

Queen looked over her shoulder at the man Allison was talking about. She sucked her teeth. "Gurl please!" She waved away the notion. "You don't know if he was talking about our Myka. Besides, if it was over between them she would have told us so."

Allison folder her arms and leaned back with a sista-girl pose. "How many Myka Ellises do you know that runs Ellis Publications?" she asked her.

Queen's eyes widened. "Gurl, for real?" she took another look at the two men at the bar. She noticed the man in question did indeed look like Ne-Yo. Queen scrutinized him, and concluded Myka couldn't have missed with that one. She also gave his friend a quick once over. Both men were prime.

Allison gladly nodded in the affirmative; happy to be the one to break the news. Queen grabbed her purse up from the table.

"What are you doing?" Allison asked, watching Queen frantically search through her knock- off Michael Kors bag.

Finally locating what she was looking for, she pulled out her phone. "I'm calling Myka!"

Allison's lips spread with the widest grinned she could muster. She thought it was an excellent idea. What better source to get conformation than the horse's mouth?

***

Nate listened while Garrett explained why he was enamored with Ms. Ellis, without missing a beat with the Double Mint twins. Ms. Nosy couldn't wait to bee-line it back across the room to her friend to share the news. He watched the dancing queen become animated at whatever news Nosy was telling her. Dancing Queen must have needed confirmation because she quickly whipped out her phone to place a call. Nate shook his head. *What a pair.*

Garrett stopped in mid sentence to turn to see what had captured Nate's attention. "What's going on?" He asked.

"Nothing, I hope," he responded. *And for those two's sake there better not be.*

Chapter 11

Derrick entered his home flinging his briefcase across the room; shattering several expensive crystal pieces that graced a table along the far wall. He was enraged.

He happened to be walking past a clothing store window when he spotted Myka with him—Garrett Pleasant; the one man he hated most in life. He stood there watching while Myka smiled and laughed as Garrett modeled the clothes he tried on. More than seeing how happy Myka seemed with the man was how Garrett looked at he. He knew that look. Garrett wanted her and that just couldn't happen. He would stop breathing before he let Garrett get in the way of his plans for Myka. When had the two met and why were they together at all? How had he missed this?

Derrick stalked to his bar to pour himself a drink. He downed it in one gulp, before reaching for the bottle to pour himself another. After gulping that down, he threw the glass with force, shattering a window.

"There is no way in hell I will let him have her. No way!" Derrick stalked around the room trying to think. How did this happen and what could he do about it? He had to stop whatever was going on between Myka and Pleasant and stop it now!

Calming himself, Derrick reached for another glass to pour a third drink. This time the warm liquid soothed him. He would stop Garrett Pleasant and have Myka back, but first he needed to have his window repaired. He placed a quick call to his on-call handyman to replace the window. It didn't matter the late hour. Derrick had done enough business with the man over the years, to have him on retainer without boundaries for time or money.

With that call placed, he cleaned up the mess he'd made with the briefcase. His mother was going to kill him. The sculptures were a gift from her for his birthday. He made a mental note to replace them before she knew they were gone. He certainly didn't need Janice Steele nagging him over a gift paid with his credit card.

Grabbing his car keys, he had a house call to make for some answers.

Chapter 12

Myka had just closed her eyes when her phone rang. "Now who is this?" Irritated, she checked the phone's display; it was Queen. She sighed. She probably wanted to ream her for missing girls' night out.

Clicking the answer button, Myka greeted her friend.

"Why didn't you tell us you broke up with Derrick?" Queen asked; foregoing the pleasantries.

How the hell does she know that? Myka frowned. "How did you find out?"

"That's not the issue. Why didn't *you* tell us?" Queen glanced over at Allison who was ear to ear with her on the phone. She mouthed: *It's true*. Allison nearly leaped into the air with the possibilities for her and Derrick.

Myka sighed. "I was going to tell you when I met you all for drinks, but as you know I had another appointment."

Hearing Myka's explanation, Allison twisted her mouth knowingly. Queen was about to tell her what they knew about that too, until Allison shook her head wildly, while making a cutting motion across her neck, preventing her from revealing their source. That was something she wanted them to keep for themselves for the time being.

Queen may have had her reasons for not telling Myka, but Allison's were to further her advancement on Derrick. She wanted to be the one to drop that little bomb. Showing him Myka never cared for him, if she could so quickly fall into the arms of another man. And if things didn't work out with Derrick, well, maybe the new man would fit the bill. She cut her eyes back across the room to the bar. The man in question was still sitting there talking with his friend.

Hanging up, Myka fell back onto her pile of pillows. She only spoke to Queen a couple of minutes, but she was exhausted. The woman was exhausting. She had to promise she would call her soon to give her the full run down on what happened to get her off the phone. Staring at the ceiling, Myka thought over her friendship with Queen. Cymone never liked her and wondered why she kept her around.

Myka met Queen a year ago when she was volunteering at a women's shelter as an outreach councilor. Queen, a resident at the time, was alone and down on her luck. When Myka would take her turn leading in some of the shelter's activities, she noticed Queen never participated. Understanding how hard change was for some of the women, she took it upon herself to befriend her. She took Queen under her wing to help her to rebuild her life. They had spent so much time together she informally became one of the girls.

Although Queen had come a long way from that beaten down woman she used to be, her true personality never changed. She was sometimes loud, raunchy and lacked self-restraint when it came to men. Myka attributed this behavior to her new found freedom from her abuser, who was killed in a shoot out with police, shortly before she left the shelter. From Myka's view, Queen was looking for attention in all the wrong places. But Cymone saw her in a different light. She said Queen was just straight ghetto and that her loose behavior was in her all the time. She pointed out that people didn't venture far from their true character.

Turning over onto her side, Myka sighed. Maybe it was time to cut the cord with Queen. It wasn't like the woman didn't have other friends she could hang out with, because she did. They found that out the hard way when Myka invited her to join them at a jazz club. Queen brought two of her home girls who were just as loud and unruly and she was. The trio was so disruptive, Myka had to pull

Queen aside and break things down to her. From there on out, Queen left her girls in the hood whenever she was invited to join her uptown friends.

Remembering that night, Myka chuckled at first then straight out laughed. She would never forget the look on Cymone's face when the hood sistas showed up. She and Allison thought she would have a stroke. That was the first and last time she and Cymone had a serious conversation about Queen. Cymone made her promise if she got out of line again she would cut her loose. And although Queen's questioning of her, as if she owed her any explanation wasn't technically considered out of line, maybe it was time to end the attachment.

Thinking of Cymone, Myka picked up the phone again to call her best friend. It was time she told her about Derrick and she meant *everything*. If she couldn't tell her best friend, who could she tell?

Chapter 13

Cymone stared at her phone as it vibrated across the countertop. She knew she should pick up, especially if Myka was calling at this hour, but she couldn't. She was still in disbelief at her predicament. She was broke. All of her money was gone. Somehow someone had gotten into her accounts and taken everything she had worked so hard for. After discovering her money had vanished, Cymone's mind immediately zeroed in on one culprit—Jamal Linden.

She got on the phone to call him only to find the number had been disconnected. She called the company he supposedly worked for, only to find out the truth. Everything he'd told her was a lie. There was no Fortune 500 job, cars or home; hell, there wasn't even a mother. After making some calls and tracking down one of his known associates, she discovered Jamal's mother had died years ago of a heart attack, after he had robbed her blind. And to top it all off, Jamal Linden wasn't even his real name. She felt so stupid. She was supposed to be smarter than this.

Cymone discovered her missing money when she pulled up one of her accounts online that morning. It had a zero balance. Panicking she pulled up another and another with the same results—zero balance. She had been on the phone all day trying to track down her funds with the only solution from the financial institutions was—hire an attorney. Everything on their end pointed to her as the person who withdrew it all. It was even indicated that the requests came from her home computer. The one person she could think of who could have done this was Jamal. He asked to use her computer once, to check his email and like a fool she let him.

No, she couldn't talk to anyone right now. How could she let her best friend know what a fool she had been. How she unwittingly allowed a man to get over on her. She was an intelligent woman. How did this happen? It wasn't like she was some desperate single mother who had her tax refund check taken by some sweet talking fool who only came around during tax season. She was an executive; *the* buyer for a chain of upscale department stores known worldwide. It was she who graduated at the top of her class. And because she had done so well in the stock market, everyone came to her for financial advice. This wasn't supposed to happen to her!

Cymone sighed as a single tear slid down her powdered cheek. That was all that she would give that son of a bitch Jamal. The next tears would be his, once she got her hands on him.

Yes. She would get an attorney and make him pay and pay dearly. If she never got one cent back, the satisfaction of seeing that lying, thieving asshole behind bars would be worth it. With that thought came the remembrance that she had access to an attorney. Cymone quickly sprang to her feet to retrieve Nate's business card from her purse.

"Nathaniel Morrison, Attorney at Law." She would contact him first thing in the morning.

Chapter 14

Tessa rolled her eyes and pulled tight the belt to her robe, as she hurried to answer her door. Someone was pounding on it like there was no tomorrow.

"Damn it, I'm coming!" She wanted to give whoever it was a piece of her mind. She had just run a nice hot bath to soothe away her disappointment in not snagging Garrett Pleasant. But there was always tomorrow, she thought, as she disengaged the lock and pulled the door open.

Before she could utter a word, Derrick grabbed her by the throat, pushing her backwards inside the apartment; all the while kicking the door close behind him. Tessa, eyes wide from the assault, clawed at his tightening fingers, as she desperately tried pulling air into her lungs.

Shoving her away from him, Derrick pointed his finger at her. "Why didn't you tell me about Garrett Pleasant," he hissed at her accusingly.

Barely maintaining her balance, Tessa coughed and spat as she finally drew a healthy breath. "What the hell are you talking about?" She clutched the collar of her robe closer to her now reddening and swelling throat. "You could have killed me!" She shouted at him.

Staring at her intently, Derrick slowly shook his head. "If I wanted you dead bitch you wouldn't be speaking right now." Tessa shrank back from his words. From the look in his eyes, he meant them.

"Garrett Pleasant," he repeated. Derrick stared her down. He wasn't going to be nice about it if he had to ask again.

She knew this was about Myka; it was always about Myka, and never about her. "I didn't think it was important. He's a client nothing more," Tessa told him, still clutching her robe to her throat.

Derrick's eyes narrowed. "A client…what do you mean a client? What business could Garrett Pleasant possibly have with Myka?"

"Garrett has written a novel and Ellis is handling the publishing."

Easing into an unnatural calm, Derrick chuckled at first, and then flat out guffawed. He laughed so hard he doubled over. "Garrett Pleasant the author." Composing himself, Derrick shook his head. "What can't that man do?" His manner quickly changed from humor back to anger. Garrett had to be the golden boy in everything.

"Actually his book is quite good. I was assigned to edit it until I showed interest in the man himself, then Myka took it away from me. She hired an outside editor to handle his precious manuscript." Tessa frowned. This was another reason to hate Myka. She knew she could have done his novel justice if given the chance.

Derrick quickly zeroed in on Tessa's interest in Garrett. He could use it to his advantage. He slowly moved towards a cautious Tessa, but this time he took her into his arms.

"I'm sorry for coming in here that way. I didn't mean to hurt you. I'm sorry."

He enclosed her tighter in his embrace before kissing the top of her head. His lips moved from there to her forehead, then down to her lips where they lingered, before pushing his tongue into her mouth. His hands moved from her back, around to the knot holding her robe closed. Undoing her belt, all the while probing her mouth with his tongue, Derrick removed the robe from her body. His hands found her breasts; kneading them until she moaned for more. Letting his left hand drift to the V at the top of her thighs, he lazily massaged her there, until she was wet and ready. Lifting Tessa up into his arms, he took her to her bedroom to make things up to her.

***

"I need you to do something for me," Derrick told a satisfied Tessa. He was gazing at her from her bedroom mirror while he buttoned his shirt. Tessa was lying in her disheveled bed watching him.

"Sure, what is it?"

"I need you to get close to Pleasant and seduce him. He has way too much interest in Myka." If anyone could get the job done Tessa could. She had proven that time and time again.

"If that's what you want baby. Anything for you." Little did Derrick know, Tessa already had plans for Garrett Pleasant. And since things were the way they were between them, why shouldn't she have a new man? And Garrett Pleasant fit the bill perfectly.

Derrick walked back to Tessa, leaning down for a kiss. "If I were capable of love, I would love you," he brazenly told her. He kissed her again before pulling on his coat to leave. He gave her a wink before exiting her bedroom.

Tessa sighed with relief. She usually didn't mind when Derrick showed up, but tonight he was more enraged than usually. He had never laid a finger on her before, and once again she had Myka to thank for that. Everything would have been fine had Myka played her part and let

Derrick have his way until he was tired of her. But no, she had to go off script and dump him. Now he became her problem. That was until she got Garrett into her bed and then things would be right between her and Derrick again.

Tessa and Derrick had an odd and rocky relationship that no one would understand, but it worked for them. They both understood they couldn't have more than shared stolen moments together, and most of the time Tessa was ok with that. But in spite of everything, she loved Derrick. He knew it and always used it to his advantage. So to remedy his rejection, Tessa looked for love wherever she could find it. Throwing herself at men like Garrett for the attention Derrick refused to give her. Somewhere deep down, she knew Garrett Pleasant didn't want her either, but she had to try. If he got to know her, he just might find it in his heart to like her.

Chapter 15

Nate leaned back into his chair in total surprise at his first appointment of the morning. It was the woman from last night. He had hoped she would call, but finding her standing in his office was something else.

Finally realizing he wasn't dreaming, he bolted from his chair to across the room to greet her. From what his assistant told him, her name was Cymone Davis. He now had a name.

"Well I must say I never expected to see you here in my office," he told her, as he guided her to the expensive leather sofa across the room.

"And I never expected to be here either," she confided. Even though she knew she had no other choice, she was still nervous about being there. She never had a reason to seek out an attorney before and certainly not one she found herself attracted to.

"What can I do for you Cymone?"

Cymone raised a brow at his forwardness. He skipped the polite handles and addressed her as if he knew her. But that was his initial intentions. He made that quite clear the night before. She could have addressed this but she decided to let it pass. She had more important things to worry about than his familiar approach to their meeting.

"Someone has stolen all of my money and I need your help in getting it back." There, she said it, it was out. She was willing to bet, after she told him her tale of woe, he would reconsider his intentions of wanting to date her. She felt like a fool and after he understood what happened and why, in his eyes, she would look like one too.

After Nate settled beside her with a legal pad and a pen, she plunged into her story; watching his facial expressions with every sentence for any disappointment or disdain. But to her surprise, he only nodded from time to time, as he scribbled page after page into his pad. He never showed any judgment or dissatisfaction against her. He just listened and made copious notes. After she finished, she held her breath for the fallout.

There was none. He asked her a few questions; wrote some more; picked up his phone to speak with his assistant then came back to sit beside her again.

"Cymone, I am going to do everything in my legal power to get you your money back," he assured her. *And maybe a few illegal things if I get my hands on this Jamal*, he added to himself.

He watched her wring her hands while she explained everything to him, and with every turn of her fingers he wanted to wring the man's neck.

Now he reached for those hands, placing both in his own. "Cymone, you did nothing wrong. It isn't your fault the man is scum. When you learned of his so-called gambling habit you dropped him. That's what you were supposed to do. He had no right to steal from you. So stop beating yourself up, ok?" He gave her hands a reassuring squeeze to relax her.

"You don't think I'm an idiot?" she asked him.

Nate shook his head. "You're not the idiot, he is. I am going to make sure he pays for what he's done to you.

Standing, he pulled her up with him. "I wish I had more time to speak with you, but I'm due in court in a little while, *and* I have to get started on your case. But I would like for you to join me for dinner soon. We'll have much to talk about." Nate caught Cymone's skepticism. "About the case Cymone, about the case."

Nate led her to the door. "My assistant has your contact information and I will call you later to arrange a meeting." Then without warning, he kissed the palm of her hand, smiling at her shock. He would let that sink in until he saw her again.

Nate really didn't have to be in court. He had to rush her out of his office before he lost it. Soon as he closed his door, he buzzed his assistant to hold his calls and then he raged at the air. If he could have had Jamal Linden in front of him at that very moment, he would hurt him something serious. No woman should have to endure what Cymone was facing. It could take months, if not years to restore everything to her. All because some greedy bastard found it easier to take what he wanted instead of working for it.

Yes, he would get her money back, even if he had to take it out of Jamal Linden' ass.

Nate composed himself and settled at his computer monitor. It was time to track this asshole down.

***

Cymone couldn't believe how easy that was. The man made her feel comfortable and relaxed throughout the whole process. Nate Morrison was nothing like she expected and she was glad. Now she had to buck up and find the courage to give Myka the news. This would be more difficult. It was one thing to tell all of your faults to a stranger and quite another to admit them to your closest friend. But tell her she would.

Chapter 16

Jamal Linden, aka Samuel Taylor, along with many other aliases, grinned when he saw the number that included all those zeros in his newly opened bank account. This was his biggest haul yet. He had funneled nearly half a million dollars from Cymone's accounts into his. He was surprised at the amount of money she possessed. Considering her fairly young age, she had done alright for herself. He had expected maybe one fifty to two hundred thousand tops.

"Not bad for a few weeks work, not bad at all," he told himself, as he closed the web browser. He had made it a habit of checking his account at least once a day, to reassure himself he had actually pulled it off.

He just loved lonely desperate women. They were so easy and so trusting. They would turn a blind eye to almost anything just to have a hard body lying next to them at night. He had to admit, Cymone wasn't as easy as most. She wasn't the mama type. When he told most women his troubles, they wanted to mother him; take him in and make things all better. But not Cymone. She wanted to get rid of him. Once he laid down his line about how he got caught up into gambling, she quickly wanted him gone.

Another passenger on the single's cruise, Jamal targeted Cymone soon after they boarded the ship. He made it a point to stay close to the group of women when he spotted them at the airport. In his experience, there were usually at least one or two women in a group who had a little money and looking for love. Singles cruises were a hustlers dream. Nothing but lonely women looking for Mr. Right or Mr. Right Now.

Once the ship sailed, he scoped out each woman in their group. Always standing just within ear shot to determine who had money and who didn't. It didn't take him long to eliminate Myka since most of her capital was tied to loans concerning her company. Queen and Allison were quickly pegged as wanna-bees, with low to medium paying jobs. So that left Cymone with her high-grossing salary, but conservative lifestyle. From what he could gather, she was all about nesting and stacking for the future, which made her the perfect target.

When they officially met, he hooked her with his fictitious job title and overwhelming sense of education and style. When he worked a degreed woman, he had to work a little harder at the lies. He had done his homework though. The employer he used in his scam actually had a Jamal

Linden working for the company, just in case she had the urge to check out his story.

It was only after a few dates, when she mentioned stopping by his house, that he 'came clean' about his gambling problem. He told her, because he made so much money on his job, he had become bored. He had bought his dream cars and his dream home, but it just hadn't been enough. So feeling the need to feel challenged, he started gambling. It was small stakes at first, but after he won most of the bets and card games, he upped the ante until he found himself over his head; losing everything except one of the luxury cars (which was on loan from his real job) and having to move back in with his mother. He fed her the usual about attending Gamblers Anonymous and how he was recovering his losses by refocusing his attention on his work.

Blah, blah, blah. Usually this is when his mark would welcome him in with open arms. But not Cymone. She was nobody's fool. If he hadn't stepped up his plans and gotten access to her computer when he had, he would have missed his payday. Cymone gave him the 'this isn't working out' speech the instant he finished 'checking his email'. That was a close call. He had to laugh though. In the end, he still was able to fleece her despite her concerns.

Jamal looked around his hotel suite. He needed to make some plans. He had hoped to remain in his apartment for a while longer, but after discovering Myka was Tessa's boss, well that was too close for comfort. It was a good thing he asked about her job before he picked her up for lunch that last day they were together. All he needed was to run into Myka and have her call the police. By now he was sure Cymone had told her everything. Those two confided in each other on every aspect of their lives, which was equally dangerous for him. It was a good thing he had been cautious where Tessa was concerned.

His only regret was having to leave Tessa. She was some hot piece of ass. He could have spent a few more weeks playing around with her. There wasn't anything that woman wouldn't do. There was no pretense with Tessa. He could be himself. It didn't matter to her that he had a minimum wage job, as long as he was good to her in bed. Tessa was exceptional, but a liability. He couldn't afford to be associated with her any longer for fear of being caught.

So he quit his Budget Rent-a-Car job and moved into one of the finer hotels until he decided on what to do next. It was time he left town, but he wanted to plan out his getaway for once and not leave on the run as he usually did. He would just lay low for the time being to get his bearings. With this colder than usually weather he was leaning toward somewhere warm and tropical.

Chapter 17

"A friend of yours?" Nate tossed a thumb over his shoulder at a retreating Tessa.

Wearing a short coat that covered close to nothing, even in the frigid weather, Tessa made sure she had everyone's attention as her hips swayed their way to the front entrance. Most of the men nearly twisted their heads from their shoulders to capture an eyeful. A couple of them colliding, while trying not to miss her dramatic exit.

Tessa had been 'coincidently' in the courthouse when she literally bumped into Garrett exiting one of the courtrooms. She made small talk, all the while touching a bicep or pec with each flirtatious sentence.

When she was finished feeling him up, she asked Garrett to lunch which he quickly, but politely declined. There was no way he was getting anywhere near Tessa Andrews alone. There was no telling what kind of trouble she could get him caught up in. And her kind of trouble he would avoid at any cost. He had to hand it to the woman. She was persistent even after Myka's talk with her. But then again, Myka couldn't control what she did on her own time. Garrett was skeptical as to why she was at the courthouse, since he could have sworn he saw her earlier in his favorite coffee house. But when he neared the spot where he thought he saw her, she was gone.

Garrett grimaced. "No she's not."

Nate chuckled. "Man you know how to pull 'em."

"No respectable man should want to pull that. The woman is a little too hungry for my taste."

There was a time he may have taken Tessa up on her offer, but that was many moons and a couple of degrees ago. He had done his fair share of plowing through women during his undergrad years, before law school. But those days were long gone.

"You got a minute? I have this client who's had her bank account picked clean by a casual acquaintance. I need some manpower to track the scum down." Nate gave Derrick the particulars in the case he was handling for Cymone. He would need the help of the D.A.'s office for the necessary resources to track Jamal down.

"I will make some calls and you'll have everything you need at your disposal," Garrett assured him.

"Thanks man." Nate clasped his shoulder before heading down the corridor towards a bank of elevators.

"No problem." Garrett glanced at his watch. It was nearly time for him to be in the courtroom for Unger's bail hearing. He had no doubt the judge would set something that was far out of the man's reach, so he wasn't worried about him making bond. In fact, this hearing perplexed him. This was Unger's second attempt at bond, first with Nate and now with his new court appointed lawyer. Why was this man wasting everyone's time? No matter what bond was set he couldn't pay it.

Checking his watch again, he had just enough time to call Myka. He hoped he could set something up for later that evening to meet with her. Hopefully dinner if she was willing.

***

Tessa was a little frustrated. She was hoping she could persuade Garrett into having lunch with her or for that matter having her for lunch, but he turned her down. Claiming he was due in court most of the day. But on the bright side, he didn't say they would never have lunch together, so that was something.

She couldn't wait to have that man trapped between her thighs. And when he experienced what she could do with her mouth, she knew for sure she would have him hooked. Having Garrett Pleasant would more than make up for the lost of her last lover—and for Derrick too for that matter.

Tessa thought of Derrick. She hadn't heard from him since their last encounter. It was just as well. Even though they were good together in bed, out of the sack, he left her wanting; always hanging on for the next time he would just show up.

Part of her wanted to be done with him, but the other part made her body tingle just thinking about him. Their whole relationship had never been about anything other than sex. In the beginning she was more than okay with their arrangement; no strings attached. But the more he came around, the more love she felt for him. A love he would never return.

Wrapping her inadequate coat tightly around her flimsy dress, she decided to grab a sandwich and head back to the office. She would find time to 'bump' into Garrett Pleasant another day.

Chapter 18

Cymone waited while Nate thumbed through some of the papers he brought with him. They were seated in a private dining room in one of her favorite Italian restaurants. She was skeptical at first when he called to have her meet him there. And when the maître d escorted her to one of its private dining areas, she was on full alert. What kind of meeting could she be having with her attorney in a private setting at a posh restaurant?

But from the moment she arrived, Nathaniel Morrison had been nothing but business. When asked about the meeting place, he simply stated he hadn't eaten all day and since his favorite dining place had private rooms, he thought they could get a meal and get some work done too. She had to admit, she found the man attractive, and if her life wasn't in such a shambles, she may have used his card to initiate a date instead of a legal consultation. But with what he told her so far, she was glad she had chosen the latter. Nate was confident that he'd found Jamal and more importantly her money.

They had just finished an excellent meal. An entrée she never knew the restaurant served. She discovered the chef was a personal friend of Nate's and only prepared the dish for him. Cymone was impressed. The man was intelligent, handsome and wealthy; and it seemed he had some influence in this town. Yes, she was duly impressed.

"Here, this is the account that I've traced your money to. I followed the cyber trail from your IP address to this bank. Mind you, it went through several different servers, but the thief isn't very sophisticated and only has basic knowledge in hiding funds. He was either too cheap to hire someone with more knowledge to do it for him or he was counting on your shame to keep you silent about the whole affair."

Nate was more than happy to catch this scumbag. And even more happy that it didn't take a lot of effort to do so. Usually with cyber crime, the criminals are so sophisticated it would take months to track them down and that was just to get a slim idea of who they were. But this thief was all about the money and not hiding.

"So what happens now?" Cymone picked up her near empty wine glass for a sip.

"I've had this account frozen and tagged, so when he logs on or tries to move the money, the action will trigger his whereabouts. I think he's still in the city because the money is still here. If he had left town there was no way he would leave it in this account." Nate watched as relief washed over Cymone. She took another drink from her glass draining it. He leaned across the table to pour her another one.

"And I know you're wondering how we're going to catch him." She nodded.

"Well from what my IT guy tells me, someone logs into this account every day, so we've placed a trap that will capture the IP address and locate the computer used to login. And soon as he does, we'll have him."

"I don't know how to thank you. You didn't have to take my case considering I don't have the funds to pay you."

"Not yet." Nate winked. He would have taken the case anyway, just because it was her.

"Yes, not yet. But I will pay you the moment my money is safely back into my account, so send me the bill." Cymone would pay him whatever he asked. The man was amazing and she told him so.

Nate smiled at her accolades. "Oh that reminds me. You need to have an entirely new account set up. Although you will have your money back that account has been compromised.

"Already done. In fact, I've even changed banks. I know they weren't at fault, but I'll just feel better knowing that it's out of Jamal's reach in case he gets away.

Nate shook his head. "I don't think you will have to worry about Jamal or whoever he's calling himself this week, ever again. The man is wanted in several states which make this a case the FBI will want. They take these types of crimes very seriously." Nate explained to Cymone that Jamal Linden was indeed an alias. And at this point, no one was sure of his true identity. He promised to let her know the moment they had him in custody.

Cymone yawned. "I'm sorry. It's been a long day." She hadn't slept much since this ordeal began and it was starting to show.

"Don't apologize. You've been through a lot. Did you drive here?"She nodded, yawning again.

"Why don't I call you a cab and have your car delivered to your home?" Nate didn't want her to drive. Even though she only had what amounted to one glass of wine, he was still cautious, because she was exhausted.

Cymone was already shaking her head, before he could finish his sentence. "That won't be necessary, I'm fine," she told him. But she wasn't; she was drained.

It was Nate's turn to shake his head no. "I insist. You're dead on your feet. And it won't be any trouble for me to have your car delivered. So grab you things while I have Tim get you a cab." Nate excused himself to track down the maitre d.

Cymone watched him leave the room. She smiled. Nate was a true gentleman. She wondered why he didn't offer to take her home. She knew he was attracted to her. She shrugged. Maybe he did change his mind after all.

This thought brought a frown. Cymone swallowed. She hoped her stupidity didn't drive the man away. She was beginning to really like him and hoped after the mess was over, they could at least be friends and hopefully more. Her thoughts were interrupted when Nate came back into the room.

"Ready?" he asked.

"Ready."

***

Once again Nate found himself watching Cymone leave. He wanted more than anything to drive her home, but he would have wanted to make sure she was safely inside. This on its own was not a problem. It was what he would want to do once inside that would be the problem.

The entire night he wanted to kiss Cymone and he knew if he took her home he would fulfill that want. This was something he promised himself he wouldn't do until after her case was solved and closed. So for now, he would just have to be satisfied with their business meetings to enjoy her company. He hoped the police caught Jamal soon.

Chapter 19

Derrick looked up from his work at the sound of the doorbell chiming. Glancing at his watch, he realized he had been working for hours. He was in his home office trying to catch up on some cases he had neglected in his pursuit of Myka. He was still smarting from finding her with Garrett.

Stretching, Derrick rose to see who was bold enough to come to his home uninvited.

***

Allison pulled the belt to her coat a little tighter while she waited for Derrick to answer his door. It was time she made her move. Myka had ventured off with another man so there was no reason she shouldn't have Derrick. She'd wanted him from the moment she saw him.

In fact, she saw him first, before Myka even knew he existed. She caught sight of him standing near them at the jazz festival. She was in awe at how handsome he was. But before she could make her move to approach him, he turned and headed in their direction. They briefly made eye contact and she gave him her sexiest smile. But instead of approaching her, he passed her to get to Myka. It was always Myka, never her.

But this time she had the upper hand. Myka didn't want Derrick and he would have to accept that, especially after she showed him what he was missing in not having her in his bed. Allison never could see what Derrick saw in Myka in the first place. She wasn't one of the friendliest people in the world. She was never one to approach men or mingle with them in a public setting like she and Queen. Even Cymone, with her high minded self, would strike up a conversation with a man, but not Myka. And she was willing to bet Myka wasn't that exciting in bed either. Allison shook her head. In her opinion, just to look at Myka indicated no fire at all.

Derrick pulled open the door. His brow furrowed at who he discovered on the other side.

"Allison?"

Allison grinned. "Hello Derrick." She hesitated before adding, "Aren't you going to invite me in?"

Not knowing what else to do, Derrick gestured for her to enter. He watched her take in his home, while he patiently waited for her to speak. He was curious to know why she was there. He didn't have to wait long.

Allison eyes swept her surroundings. She was impressed at what she saw. Derrick Steele was doing alright for himself. She thought Myka was a fool for leaving all of this. She gave the space another sweep before turning back to Derrick.

"I heard you and Myka were no longer together and I just wanted to drop by to see if you were okay. I know how much you liked her and for the record, I think the woman is a fool for dropping someone as hot as you." Allison didn't mince her words. She wanted him to know she was interested and he wouldn't have to play any games to get her.

A corner of Derrick's mouth lifted into a knowing grin as he stared at the woman before him. With all the expressive looks and the intentional banter whenever she was around, he should have expected her. But the thought never crossed his mind that Allison would be 'that' friend women had to watch around their man. If Myka thought she had an ally in this one, she was sadly mistaken. He let his gaze casually sweep over her. She wasn't bad looking, and if he hadn't set his sights on Myka, he would have taken some time to play with her for awhile.

He knew Allison was attracted to him when he met them all in St. Lucia. She couldn't take her eyes off of him, and was more than a little disappointed when he chose Myka over her. Now that she found he and her friend were no longer involved, she couldn't wait to throw her hat in the ring. The woman made it perfectly clear as to why she was there. And from the looks of her, she had no intentions of leaving without what she came for. Well if she wanted him, he would make sure she got him, at least for the night.

Without saying another word, Derrick pulled Allison towards him by the belt that held her coat closed. He took his time to untie the knot she had tied there. After freeing the coat from its belt he pushed the opening apart to discover she was completely naked underneath. He quickly relieved her of the covering.

Allison smiled knowingly. She never expected things to move this fast. She expected to have to convince him she was the one he needed. But this was good too. In fact, it was better than good; it was wonderful. She knew Derrick was what she had been looking for all along. Someone who would take charge; a man who knew how to handle a real woman.

Allison moaned when he lowered his head to capture a hardened nipple with his mouth. She pressed his head to her other breast when he came up for air. After giving her full breasts the attention they deserved, Derrick swept Allison up into his arms and carried her to the nearest sofa. Stripping himself of his clothing, he settled himself inside her for the rest of the evening.

***

Hours later, Allison pulled on her coat while Derrick placed more wood on the fire. Although she was smiling, she felt no joy; she was actually fuming inside. After they made initial contact on the sofa, he moved them to the plush rug in front of the fireplace, where they spent the remainder of their time pleasing each other. Everything was great until Derrick called her Myka.

Allison was floored. She had come there to make him forget about Myka only to have the man think of her while he was pumping away inside of her.

Myka, Myka, Myka. Was she all these men ever thought of? Not only did she still have Derrick fawning all over her, she had this new man, this attorney, falling all over himself too. What was is it about Myka!

Derrick came up from behind to snuggle against her. "Babe you were great." And he meant it. Allison had something to prove and by all accounts she had done her job and done it well. He was seriously considering trading Tessa in for her. At any rate, he would definitely see her again. Kissing her a final time he led her to the door.

Derrick gave her one of his cards. "Call my cell so I will have your number."

Allison genuinely smiled and nodded. *At least he's willing to see me again. If he thought I was good tonight, he will be out of his mind when I get through with him the next time. And I'll make sure he never utters Myka Ellis' name ever again.*

***

Derrick chuckled and shook his head after letting Allison out. Women never ceased to amaze him. They were always going on and on about men not treating them right. Why would they, if women were always throwing themselves at men like him. Allison was supposed to be Myka's good friend, but she couldn't wait to open her legs for him. And he would let her do just that until he was tired of her. He just hoped she didn't think he would forget about Myka. He still planned to get her back into his bed. And if Allison still wanted to stick around, well, he could handle that too. It was no slip of the tongue, when he called out Myka's name. He wanted Allison to know that Myka was forefront in his mind and would be until he squared things with her.

A devious smile crept across his face. He wondered what Myka would think if she knew her so-called friend had shown up at his home practically naked, ready and willing to do whatever he asked? Had he known Allison was coming, he would have videotaped their encounter, just for Myka.

Women. As long as they acted the way they did, men like him would be taking full advantage of them.

Derrick yawned. It was time he got some sleep. He had big things planned for tomorrow.

Chapter 20

Garrett walked into his office and slammed the door. He couldn't believe the day he'd had. First, one of the rookie officers had forgotten to read a killer his Miranda rights, which led to him waltzing out of court as if he had won the lottery. Then if that wasn't enough, Jason Unger was released that afternoon on bond.

He couldn't believe it. He expected the judge to set bail and set it high enough that there was no way he would walk, and Judge Clemons did not disappoint. Bail was set at two million dollars, much higher than the first bond. He had gone to bed that night knowing there was no way in hell Unger could come up with that kind of cash, especially if he couldn't bond out the first time. But all of that had been thrown out the window when he was leaving the courthouse today. His assistant called to inform him the bond had been paid anonymously.

Garrett was livid. The one sure thing had blown up in his face. He had many questions. He had to find out who was stupid enough to risk a two million dollar bond to set Unger free; knowing he may, at the very least skip town, or at the worst finish what he started—killing his wife and child. Who could Unger know with that kind of money to throw around? But there was a bigger question. Why didn't the person pay the first bail which was much cheaper?

Garrett rubbed his temples; a headache was trying to settle there. Although he needed to take something to stop it in its tracks, it would have to wait. He needed to arrange protection for the man's wife and son. Unger would no doubt try to track them down and he wouldn't put it past him to show up at the hospital to finish the job on his wife. Even though he tried his best to put an end to her life, Patricia Unger had beat all odds and survived. Her son was placed in foster care while she healed.

After securing Patricia and her son's safety, Garrett finally dropped into his chair. He didn't need this right now. It was the beginning of winter and things usually slowed down for the criminal justice department. Unlike in the heat of summer, it was usually too cold for criminals to be out and about making mayhem. Everyone that wanted a warm place for the winter had already committed their petty crimes to be in out of the elements. But with Unger roaming around, that peace was shattered. He had no doubt the man would try something.

Garrett had planned to spend as much time as he could on finishing the final draft of his book *and* making Myka Ellis his.

The thought of wanting Myka in his life surprised him. It had come when they were shopping for his new wardrobe. Before her, the thought of wanting someone wasn't even a flicker of a possibility. Never had he wanted a woman as much as he wanted Myka. And never had he wanted one to stick around for the long haul.

The night they shopped, he watched her as she deftly swept through the stores they visited; pulling together outfits. He had to admit, her choices may not have been his idea of doable, but once he tried on the clothes she chose for him, he was impressed. The clothing gave him a whole different look; a more rugged appeal; a bad boy persona and he liked it. He liked it because this was how she saw him.

He thought she even surprised herself when he came out of the dressing room wearing jeans and a pullover sweater that hugged his well defined chest. She had raised an eyebrow when he stood before her. Her look of wonder soon spread into a fully fledged smile. She liked what she saw. He bought everything she suggested and then some. While she was taking a call from another client, he ordered flowers to be sent to her office to thank her. He checked his watch. They should be arriving within the hour. This was his bright glimmer of light in what had started as a gloomy day. He had every intention of making Myka Ellis his no matter what it took. He just hoped she was ready for the ride.

Garrett checked his watch again; he had just enough time. He had an idea. Grabbing his briefcase he stalked from his office slowing down just enough to tell his assistant he was gone for the day. Jason Unger was out on bond and there wasn't anything he could do about it until the man did something to land himself back in jail.

But in the meantime, he was taking this time to court Myka Ellis.

Chapter 21

There were two huge bouquets of flowers sitting on her desk when she came back into her office. One more beautiful than the other. Myka didn't have to ask who they were from. The annoyance displayed on Tessa's face told it all. They had to be from Garrett.

Plucking the envelope from the arrangement nearest her, Myka read the card. Yes it was from Garrett; expressing his gratitude for the other night. She leaned into the fragrant bouquet to take a sniff. They smelled wonderful. Before she could lift the card to the second bouquet, her cell rang. Without bothering to check the caller display, she answered it; sure it would be Garrett inquiring about the flowers. But to her dismay, it was Derrick on the other end instead.

"I hope you liked the flowers I sent," he said without preamble.

Myka now knew the second vase of flowers was from Derrick. She could have kicked herself for not checking the caller-id.

She sighed before she answered. "Derrick, why are you sending me flowers?" She was becoming weary of this game he insisted on playing. She wished the man would get it into his head that she wanted nothing more to do with him.

"Well, they are a precursor for us having lunch today. I will pick you up within the hour." He felt confident. But what he really needed to know was Tessa's progress with Garrett. He needed to knock him out of the running for a clear path back into Myka's good graces.

"Well then you've wasted your money. I won't have lunch with you, because you and I are done Derrick and I wish you would accept that fact. Now if you don't mind, I would like to get back to work." She didn't give him time to rebut her rejection. She ended the call, hoping this was the final conversation she would have with the man.

Gladly tossing the phone onto her desk, she moved to the flowers Derrick sent and promptly dropped them into the trash without reading the card. It had nothing to say but old news. Nodding at her handy work, Myka glanced at her watch. She could get at least an hour or two of work done before having a late lunch, which she planned to order in. But before she could settle in at her desk, there was a knock on her door. Myka sighed, expecting more of Tessa's foolishness. But when she asked the visitor to come in, it was Garrett.

***

Derrick's mouth tightened. He couldn't believe she had the nerve to hang up on him. This was not something he was used to, not at all. Myka Ellis was beginning to grate on his nerves. He had never had to work so hard to get any woman's attention and that perplexed him as much as it angered him. Even though her rebuffs made him crazy, it also made him more determined to get her back; to make her pay for his discomfort. In his eyes, no woman had the right to deny him anything.

He picked up the phone to call her back, but thought better of it. She would only ignore the call. He was beginning to wonder if she really meant to have him out of her life. There had to be something he could do to change her mind. One way or another Myka Ellis was going to comply with his wishes. No woman had the right to walk away from him without consequences.

Chapter 22

Jason Unger smacked his lips at having his first taste of country fried steak as a free man again. He had only been locked up a few days, but he was glad to be free none the less.

When a guard called his name for court, he questioned why he had to go through the bail process again. The attorney explained, since he claimed he didn't get a fair shake with his previous attorney, he had a right to a new bail hearing just the same. Jason only shrugged. It didn't matter the amount, because there was no one to bail him out. And he certainly didn't have any money. In his opinion, it was a total waste of time.

So it was no surprise when he was led back to his cell after the judge set the ridiculous bond amount. He was prepared to spend his time in county lockup until the trial. But this morning, he could have kissed his attorney when he came to see him with the news. He didn't know how it happened, but some generous soul put up the money to have him released. When he inquired as to who could have done such a thing, he was told his bond had been paid by an anonymous source. After changing into his street clothes and retrieving his personal belongings, Jason discovered his donor was even more generous. Among his things were five hundred dollars cash and a prepaid cell phone; neither were in his possession when he was arrested.

Jason shoved some mashed potatoes with gravy into his already full month and grinned. At this point, he didn't care where the money or the phone came from, as long as he was free. He equally didn't care that the poor sap would lose every dime he put up for bail, because he had no intentions of ever showing for trial. As soon as his work was finished, he was leaving town for good.

Scanning the packed room for his waitress, he spotted his former so-called lawyer enjoying his own meal. Chewing slowly, he studied the man. Clean cut, well dressed and not a care in the world. He considered changing all that, because the man had no intentions of helping him beat the charges. He bet he and that prosecutor had already planned his fate before he even entered the room. Well he had every intentions of keeping his promise to square things with them both. But the first stop on his list of things to do was to find out more about his wife. If that bitch wasn't dead, she would soon wish she was.

Still eyeing Nate, Jason swallowed a lump of his meal; washing it down with the lemonade the waitress finally made time to deliver. Yes, he had plans and he would start immediately.

Chapter 23

"So this is why you wouldn't have lunch with me," Derrick nodded his head towards an instantly defensive Garrett. Anytime Derrick Steele appeared, it was never a good thing.

Garrett had persuaded Myka to dine with him instead of ordering food in. When he entered her office, he noticed the flowers he sent on her desk, along with those in the trash can. He wanted to ask about them, but felt he had no right to. But still he wondered. Now that Derrick Steele was standing at their table, he didn't have to wonder any longer.

Color drained from Myka's face. She thought she'd made it perfectly clear that she didn't want anything more to do with him, yet here he stood, and she wasn't pleased. One look at Garrett and she knew he wasn't pleased either.

"Derrick, what are you doing here?" Garrett ground out the question before Myka could part her lips.

"I'm having lunch." He nodded towards a group of men across the room, knowing full well it wasn't the answer Garrett was looking for.

Myka glanced in that direction. She assumed the group were either clients or from his office. She was a little relieved. It crossed her mind he may have been following her. She was sure he didn't take too kindly to her hanging up on him.

Smugly, Derrick smiled at Garrett's jaw tightening. "I spotted Myka and just wanted to say hello; *and* to ask why she would turn down lunch with me for you. You were never the better man in any situation and I think we have already established that." Derrick's eye's bore into Garrett's; challenging him.

At the men's seemingly controlled exchange, Myka became unease; her gaze swinging from one man to the other. They knew each other. Myka silently chided herself. *Of course they knew each other. As big as Metro City is, it still couldn't isolate two people who were in the same profession. And from their derision they loathed each other.*

Her heart sank. She wondered if Garrett would lose interest in her after he discovered she and Derrick were once involved. She truly hope not. She was beginning to get use to the idea of having him around and not just during business hours.

Starring back at Derrick, Garrett took his napkin from his lap and tossed it onto the table. There was no way he was going to let Derrick Steele ruin their lunch.

"Don't get up. I think I've made my point to the both of you. Enjoy your meal." With that, Derrick strolled across the crowded restaurant to his table. He only glanced their way once more, before joining the group's conversation.

"Garrett, I am so sorry about that. I've been trying to shake him for the past few weeks. He knows it's over but just won't let it go." She knew she owed Garrett an explanation, but before she could explain more he stopped her.

"No Myka, you don't have to apologize. I know how Derrick Steele works. If you dumped him, his ego won't allow him to accept that fact. How long did you two date?" It didn't matter to Garrett, but he needed to know what he was up against and how to handle it.

Myka sighed. "We dated for nearly four months; that was about all I could take of him. I met him on a singles cruise and I've been wishing ever since that I had stayed home instead." Myka felt sick. Every time she thought she had rid herself of Derrick Steele, he returned like a bad penny.

Garrett noticed her distress and reached across the table to grasp her hand. "It's ok. I do understand. That man has a way of making us both feel regret."

"How do you know Derrick? I know your paths must have crossed because of your profession, but…" She let this trail off. She wanted to know what Derrick had done to get under Garrett's skin. The man seemed unflappable up until this point.

Garrett rubbed his chin. "Well, Derrick and I, and another friend of ours, Nate, were once close as brothers when we attended law school together. Nate and I still are."

He sighed over those by gone days. "Anyway, you asked me once about me dating seriously. There was this girl, who I was very fond of, maybe even loved, and Derrick knew it. But instead of supporting the relationship as Nate had, he made it his business to wreck it. To make a long story short, I walked in on him and my girlfriend in bed together. And to make matters worse, she left me for him, until he beat her one night and she came running to me for help. I helped her." He paused and shrugged as if it were no big thing. "After she told me what happened, I encouraged her to press charges against Derrick. But when the police got involved, she claimed she had been mugged. From that point on, I haven't had anything to do with either of them."

Myka scoffed. "Is that what he meant by being the better man, by betraying you?"

Garrett nodded. He, like Myka, couldn't believe the man actually thought that way. If sleeping with his best friend's girl and beating on her made Derrick the better man, then he would gladly concede. The man was delusional indeed.

This brought another concern to mind. "Did he ever lay a hand on you?" If he had, he would march right over and beat Derrick Steele to a bloody pulp.

Myka shook her head. "No, nothing like that. But looking back, there were times when I think he wanted to hit me, especially after I broke things off."

Garrett nodded. He gave her hand another reassuring squeeze. He was in her life now, and he would do whatever it took to protect her from Derrick Steele.

Chapter 24

Jason Unger strolled from the elevator with a bouquet of his wife Patricia's favorite flowers, Persian buttercups. He was in a great mood. He was out of jail and nothing was going to stop him from carrying out his mission of revenge. He hummed a happy tune as he round the corner to the nurse's station. The young woman stationed there was very helpful in providing Patricia's room number. Clutching the flowers with anticipation, he made his way down the corridor leading to her room, only to be stopped short when he saw the two police officers stationed there.

"Damn!" It never occurred to him she would be under protection. He knew that D.A. was behind this. Jason ground his teeth. He bet the moment the judge set him free the bastard went into protection mode. Shifting his focus, he wondered where his son was. Raising the flowers to conceal his face, he continued on past the two cops.

"Hey, how's she doing?" One of them nodded towards the closed door

His partner briefly glanced at the man with the flowers before answering. "She'll live. Her bastard of a husband did some damage, but it wasn't life threatening. I overheard one of the nurses say it could have been a whole lot worse. She should be released in a day or so."

"That soon? Wasn't she burned?"

He shrugged. "You know how this works. If you're not maimed or have something blown off, they patch you up and send you on your way. They need the bed for more serious patients." He shrugged again.

"Well somebody needs to set the husband's ass on fire so he can get a taste of how it feels. How can somebody do that to another human being, and while she was holding a baby at that?" The man shook his head.

"Man, there are some evil people walking this earth. I'm just glad they're both ok and safe."

The other man shook his head. "Safe for now. That fool is out, and he may want to finish what he started."

"How right you are," Jason muttered to himself, as he moved farther down the hallway; trashing the flowers in the nearest bin. He took the stairs down to the ground floor and out to the street. He would have to find some other way to get to his wife. But while he came up with a plan, he would take the opportunity to pay the D.A. a visit. He was the reason he couldn't get to his wife and child.

Jason Unger had no qualms about snuffing out the life of either his wife or son. He never wanted any children and made that point clear before he and Patricia were married. He didn't need a greedy little mouth taking her time away from him. Patricia was his possession. His to do with as he pleased. She was to be there for him at his every beck and call; cooking, cleaning and servicing him with sex whenever he wanted it, which for Patricia's sake wasn't that often. Those were her only duties and he liked it that way.

When she told him she was pregnant, he tried beating the child from her body but the boy hung on as if to defy him. When Patricia went into labor, he refused to take her to the hospital or call an ambulance. He wanted his son to die in her womb. But she made such a fuss with all the screaming from the pain, the neighbors called the police. That was the only time the police had come to their apartment.

Whenever he would beat Patricia, he would shove a wash cloth into her mouth to muffle her cries. And no one would have been the wiser how he kept his wife in line, if she hadn't run off to the police station all bloody and bruised a couple of times. But he put a stop to that. After the second trip, he beat her so badly, she was unable to stand, let alone walk for weeks. He couldn't have her making trouble for him.

Unger sneered. Now she was holed up in a hospital room, making even more trouble. It was time to put the bitch out of her misery along with her precious child.

Chapter 25

Cameron Rogers stood at Tessa's desk squinting at her. Something was up with Ms. Thing and he wanted the dirt. Tessa was on the phone at the moment trying to ignore him, but was unsuccessful since he was making comical faces to break her concentration.

Finally released from her call, she burst into laughter. "Honey you have to stop distracting me when I'm talking to customers. The Iron Maid has already torn me a new one for flirting with one of her precious clients," Tessa told him with a mock frown.

"Do tell honey, do tell." Cameron made room on the corner of her desk to plant his wide behind. He wanted all the juice.

Cameron owned an exclusive day spa located on the floor above Ellis Publications. He and Tessa became fast friends the moment they met on the elevator two years ago when Tessa joined Myka's team. He had christened himself Tessa's personal stylist, after she made the mistake of allowing a less reputable salon to color her hair. He fussed the entire time it took to correct the mess.

Tessa leaned forward and dropped her voice. "The fine and very eligible A.D.A Garrett Pleasant swaggered in here looking all hot and gorgeous. Well, you know me being me had to let him know I was interested. Then Miss High and Mighty calls me into her office to chastise me about 'professionalism'." She made quotation marks with her fingers. "It wasn't like I had undressed for the man or anything. It was all innocent fun."

Cameron was all but oozing over this tidbit of information. He knew exactly what she meant. He had the pleasure of laying eyes on the man himself and Tessa was right on point. Too bad the man was straight.

"There wasn't anything innocent about what you did." This came from Mark who had arrived in the lobby. Frowning, Tessa folded her arms while Cameron rolled his eyes.

"Mark you are such a spoil sport. You need to loosen up a bit. The girl was only trying to have a little fun. You know how we girls like to have our fun." Cameron cackled at his own joke.

"Cameron, don't you have some hair to tease or something?" Mark asked gruffly.

"I can take a hint." He winked a Tessa. "We'll talk later." Cameron removed his bulk from her desk and sauntered off to the elevators.

"Tessa, what did Myka ever do besides give you a job and try to be halfway decent to you?" Mark was tired of her disrespect, not only of Myka but the work place in general. If Tessa wasn't talking on the phone, she was spending time downstairs in the lobby looking for new men to sleep with. He thought her behavior was disgusting.

Tessa wrinkled her nose at Mark. "I have a question for you. Why do you care how I treat Myka? It's. None. Of. Your. Business," she taunted him. With that, Tessa hopped from her chair and headed for the break room.

Mark sighed out his frustration. He actually had feelings for Tessa. He just hated the way she carried herself. He wished she would come to her senses and tone it down. In his opinion, the woman wasn't all that bad; she just needed to make some changes in her life. And she needed to start with a makeover. The clothes she wore were strictly trash. She wore too much make up and she needed to put an end to her raunchy behavior.

When she threw herself at him, he didn't take her up on the offer, because he was put off by her advances. He wanted her to act like the lady he knew she could be with the right man. He was that man, and one day he was going to sit her down and make that known. But in the mean time, he needed a strategy. He wanted to know what caused her to be the way she was. Was it a bad childhood, home life or did something happen to her recently to make her self-esteem hit rock bottom?

Mark found Tessa intelligent and confident, especially when it came to her work ethic. She was an excellent editor and would go far in the industry. But he felt something or someone was controlling Tessa and whatever it was, robbed her of her self-worth; leading her to seek the wrong type of attention. He wanted to show her how a man should love and treat a woman. Something he knew she knew nothing about. But when the time came, he would show her how love was supposed to feel.

Giving up for now, he headed to his office to get started on an author's book trailer.

Chapter 26

Myka was typing away at her keyboard when Queen burst through her door. Tessa was either not at her desk or she just let her waltz right in. She would bet it was the latter. The woman didn't have much to do with her after their talk. She stopped herself from rolling her eyes.

"Queen, what are you doing here?"

"I couldn't wait until you got around to me, I'm worried about you. What happened with you and Derrick?" Without being asked, Queen pulled up a chair to Myka's desk and placed her face in both palms waiting on an answer.

Queen could have cared less about Derrick. Personally, she was glad he was gone. He took up too much of Myka's time that should have been spent with her friends. That's how her violent relationship started. Hakeem, Queen's abusive ex-boyfriend, isolated her from her family and friends, until she had no one to turn to when he started hitting her. She didn't want that to happen to Myka.

Myka sighed. She was supposed to call Queen days ago. She had been so wrapped up in side stepping Derrick, and helping Garrett with his book, she had totally forgotten.

She knew the woman meant well, but her showing up at her office unannounced left Myka a little put off. She had to take Queen in doses and at the office was not the place for her smothering concern.

Ever since Myka befriended Queen, the woman idolized her. There was nothing too good for Myka Ellis. And when she made her a part of her family of friends with Cymone and Allison, Queen was over the moon. She never had friends as sophisticated as Myka and Allison and well, Cymone too; even though she knew Cymone couldn't stand her. So now that she had broken it off with Derrick, Queen wanted to know if there was anything she could do to help.

"Queen it just didn't work out is all. We weren't compatible. And I'm fine with it." There was no way she was going to tell her anything close to the truth about what really happened between them. Queen was far too concerned with her as it was. Any truth to be given would be to Cymone and no one else.

Queen sat up and eyed Myka carefully. Looking for any trace of sadness or grief. Satisfied there was none, she nodded her head. "You know gurl, if he put his hands on you, you know I gotchu, right?" Queen may not have been able to defend herself from her own abuser, but now that he was dead, she felt she could take on the world, especially on Myka's behalf.

Myka smiled. "Yes Queen I know. Now will you get out of here and let me get my work done. And speaking of work. Don't you have a job you should be doing?"

Queen's eyes shifted then. She didn't want to talk about that. Her latest employer let her go a week ago. The owner caught her stealing clothes from her boutique. Queen didn't think the woman would miss the few things she took. The clothes were expensive and even with her employee discount it would take her several paychecks to purchase the things she took. She just wanted a few nice things like Myka had. She wanted to fit in and knock Cymone down a peg or two. If she wore the same clothes and adopted the same style as the others in the group, maybe Cymone wouldn't hate her so much.

"You're right I do need to be there. Will you call me later?" She asked, as she headed for the door. And with that she swept out just as abruptly as she swept in.

Myka tapped a finger nail on her desk. Something was wrong. When she mentioned Queen's job, her entire attitude changed. Picking up the phone, she called Brianna, a friend who gave Queen a job as a favor to her. After patiently enduring the greetings they gave each other,

Myka asked Brianna about Queen. Brianna gave her the rundown. After learning of Queen's behavior and subsequent firing, Myka promised to do lunch and hung up.

That was the last straw. Cymone was right. Queen had to go. After all she'd done for the woman, she paid her back like this? It was a good thing Brianna was a friend or Queen would have landed herself in jail. Myka promised to pay Brianna back every penny of the total value of what Queen took from her.

Myka sighed. "No good deed goes unpunished." With the decision made to terminate their friendship, she turned back to her work. She wanted to get as much done as she could before meeting Cymone for lunch.

Chapter 27

Cymone and Myka hugged each other when they met in front of the restaurant. They chatted away about the weather and other happenings in their city, while they waited for their table. Once seated and orders placed, Cymone spoke first.

"Myka I messed up," she told her best friend. Cymone invited Myka to lunch to tell her everything, but now that the time had come, she could barely look at her; she was so ashamed. She understood what Nate told her, that it wasn't her fault, but she still felt guilty for falling for Jamal in the first place. And she knew exactly why she had.

It was her shallowness that brought this trouble to her life. She always judged people, especially men, by their careers and bank accounts, never wanting to deal with any man who didn't have at least as much as she had. She found it ironic that now she was the one who had nothing. Once this mess was over, Cymone vowed to change, and never disregard people because of her own insecurities.

Growing up, her family had been extremely poor. So much so that when she landed her first real job after college, she vowed to never be broke again. She was so hung up on this mantra, she refused to associate herself with anyone who looked poor. She never wanted to be reminded of her past pain and had worked hard to make sure it was forgotten. But here she was, right back where she started, with not a penny to her name. Thank God for credit cards or she wouldn't be having lunch with her best friend today.

"Messed up. Messed up how?" Myka stopped eating the salad their server had placed in front of her.

Cymone bit her lower lip before she answered. She was having second thoughts about telling her, but pressed forward anyway. It was better out than in, as her mother always used to say.

"Myka, I'm broke." Cymone let that sink in, before she launched into the whole story. She explained of discovering her accounts had been wiped out and how Jamal had used her computer to do it. She explained how she met Nate Morrison and hired him to retrieve her money, along with her dignity. She just hoped her friend wouldn't judge her too harshly. She had done enough of that already.

Myka pushed her plate aside. She was enraged that Jamal had done such a thing to her. Like Nate, she wanted to get her hands on him and beat him senseless.

"Oh honey, I am so sorry. You should have called me. Does Nate think he can help you?"

Cymone nodded. "Yes, he's working with the police and the bank to track the bastard down. I just hope they can catch him before my money disappears forever. He seems confident in accomplishing both. If not, I'm back to square one again."

Cymone knew Nate would do everything in his power to make it happen. She could feel it. It had been a couple of days since they talked, and for some reason Jamal hadn't logged into the account. But he was still hopeful they would catch him. Nate assured her at the very least they would be able to retrieve her funds even if Jamal was to somehow slip away. But the goal was to catch him in the act.

"You know what's mine is yours. I have a little money tucked away and I will help you until you get back on your feet."

"I appreciate that. Under any other circumstances, I would turn you down." Cymone felt bad. She wanted to refuse Myka's help, but she didn't have a choice. Nate was even waving his fee until he recovered her money. She felt like a failure.

As if reading her mind, Myka reached across the table to squeeze her hand. She felt bad for Cymone. She knew it was hard for her to reveal what happened, and even harder to accept her help. After listening to her story, it made what she had to say about Derrick a non-issue. But she would tell her just the same, if for nothing more than to get it off her chest.

She released a deep cleansing breath before launching into her own story. "Well this makes what I wanted to tell you about Derrick seem stupid."

It was Cymone's turned to be concerned. "What's the matter?" Lunch forgotten she waited for Myka to reveal her issues with Derrick.

"We broke up or should I say I ended things." Myka patted at her hair as she talked. "Derrick is manipulative and just an all around bastard, not to mention he has a weird relationship with his mother."

Cymone leaned forward. "How so?"

Myka tells her about their dates with his mother tagging along. How their supposed alone time would still manage to somehow include her. She tells her of how they would plan something only for him to do the total opposite without explanation.

"It was little things at first. It would be something as simple as asking me what I wanted for lunch only to bring me something different, stating he thought I would like it better. Constantly teasing me with one thing, only to do a switcheroo and give me something else. He acts like a con artist."

"Bait and switch," Cymone commented.

Myka nodded. She goes on to tell her about his so-called proposal and how she never saw the ring again. She explained the lunch she had with Garrett and how Derrick, uninvited, accosted them at their table. She told her how she met Garrett and how Derrick and Garrett knew each other, along with their troubled past. She also mentioned Derrick's violent demeanor which she felt was just under the surface. She felt it was only a matter of time before he gave her a taste of his aggressive temper had she not gotten away from him.

Once she finally voiced all of her concerns, Myka realized she made the right decision to break things off and not a moment too soon. Especially after talking to Garrett.

"Girl, here we were too embarrassed to tell one another our woes when we could have been consoling each other. Let's make a promise. Never to keep things like that from each other again."

Myka nodded. "Agreed."

Pulling her lunch back to her, Cymone began to eat. Her appetite had returned. Myka did the same.

Chewing on her lasagna, Cymone was curious. "I hope you didn't mention any of this to Allison or your new best friend Queen." She liked Allison well enough, but Queen was a different story. Some things they needed to keep just between the two of them.

Myka swallowed a bite of her beef before rolling her eyes. She told Cymone about her showing up at her office unexpectedly.

"You were so right. I think it's time I cut Queen loose. The woman has become too clingy and too nosy for my taste. I like her and didn't mind helping her out." Myka shook her head. "But now, I don't know." She would have to find a way to slide her out of her life gently. She didn't want to hurt the woman's feelings.

Cymone pointed her fork at her. "I told you something was off with that crazy girl and don't get me started on the way she speaks and dresses." Cymone rolled her eyes.

Myka grimaced. "That brings me to my next concern. You remember my friend Brianna, who I asked to hire her?" Cymone nodded. "Well, after I asked Queen about her job and she rushed out of my office in a hurry, I called Brianna. She caught Queen stealing from her and let her go."

Cymone nearly choked with indignation. "After all you've done for that heffa! OMG! If I were Brianna I would have had the thieving cow arrested. Yes, you turn that ungrateful bitch a loose today!" Cymone lowered her voice after she realized she was drawing attention. "And don't you dare wait another minute. If you don't want to do it, I will be more than happy to." She couldn't believe the nerve of the woman. She knew Queen was bad news the moment she met her.

Myka shook her head. "That won't be necessary; I will take care of it." How she was going to take care of it was the problem.

***

Queen's eyes watered over the conversation she just over heard.

She and a couple of her girls had entered the restaurant and she needed to wash her hands before they were seated. On the way back from the ladies room she spotted Myka and Cymone. She was about to walk over to say hello when she heard her name mentioned. Ducking behind a column she listened to the conversation.

So Myka didn't want her around anymore. That hurt. She knew Cymone had it in for her, but Myka surprised her. Well, if that's the way she wanted it, fine. Neither of them would ever hear from her again. She only wanted to be a friend and look out for the woman who looked out for her. But if she didn't want her as a friend anymore, so be it.

Queen had lost her appetite. Instead of heading back to her friends, she turned on her heels and headed for the back exit. She would text her girls once she got to her car. She didn't want to be in the same place as people who didn't want her in their life.

Chapter 28

Garrett stood looking out his window, fuming. No one had a clue where Jason Unger was. According to the man's neighbors, He had only been back to his apartment once since being released from county lockup. That meant he could be anywhere.

He was concerned, because Unger's wife Patricia was well enough to be discharged from the hospital. She had taken her son and moved in with relatives while she figured out what to do next with her life. She wanted to leave town but was needed to testify against her husband. With him not knowing the whereabouts of Unger posed a real problem. Garrett knew if Patricia was afraid, she may not testify, leaving her sick spouse open to finish the job next time.

Garrett liked it better if they had eyes on the man, hoping if Patricia felt safe, she wouldn't hesitate to put her abusive husband away this time. But at the moment, the best he could do was to maintain her surveillance.

"Knock, knock."

Garrett looked around to find Nate standing in his doorway.

"You don't look happy," Nate told him; coming fully into the office.

"I'm not. The police can't find Jason Unger. His wife was released from the hospital yesterday and now she doesn't feel safe."

"Can you blame her? The man is a lunatic. Do you think he will try and go after her?"

"With that man, I won't put anything past him." Garrett was genuinely concerned for Unger's wife and child. Nothing said he wouldn't hurt them if he had the chance.

"Ok, let me ask you another question. Do you think he means to carry out *any* threats he's made, including the ones against the both of us?"

Nate wanted a heads up if he was in danger. Initially he didn't care about the threat against himself, but he worried about Cymone. Because of the case, they had been seeing quite a bit of each other. Even though their meetings were strictly business, anyone on the outside looking in may think there was more. Especially if they could see just how over the top he was for her.

Garrett rubbed is chin. He had forgotten about that. Over the course of his career he'd received many death threats, but none ever carried out. But with Unger, he didn't know if that would be the case this time. He wanted to tell Nate he had nothing to worry about, but Unger was psycho.

"I think you may want to start carrying," he told him. His friend nodded.

Garrett was going to be taking his own advice. His life now included Myka and there was no way he would let anything happen to her.

He was just about to ask Nate to join him for an early dinner, to discuss the matter further, when his phone rang. He held up a finger to indicate Nate should wait for him.

"Pleasant." What the caller said, had him slamming down the phone and racing from his office with Nate on his heels.

***

Eyes wide, Jason Unger stood in disbelief. He was hidden in the shadows of a stand of trees, while he watched the house his wife and son were in, burn to the ground. He arrived just as the fire trucks screeched to a stop, with firemen pouring from their pumper trucks, rushing to put out the flames.

He slowly shook his head in bewilderment. He wanted to know how this happened. He only learned of his wife's whereabouts thirty minutes ago through an anonymous source via a text message on his new cell phone. And in the time it took to drive across town, the house had caught fire. He heard one of the firemen say that it wasn't an accident. Both exits had been barricaded, meaning it was set intentionally.

Someone had robbed him of the satisfaction of watching Patricia squirm before he ended her life. Yes he had great plans for her. He wanted to be up close and personal when she took her last breath, not this. He wondered who could have done such a thing. Did the people Patricia was holed up with have enemies or was this the work of his new found friend on the other end of the text?

Jason began to get an uneasy feeling at this turn of events. Was his new friend taking care of his problems for him? He didn't know. But if so, at what price? One thing was for certain, the fire had put a whole new spin on things. If someone was taking care of his problems, he needed a plan to stay one step ahead of them if he wanted his revenge on the two lawyers.

As he contemplated his new dilemma, Garrett and Nate pulled up to the scene. This piqued new interest for Jason. It was interesting that the two arrived in the same car. It was just as he thought. They had been working together all along to put him away. And with this new development, there was no doubt in his mind they would think he did this. And since they were gunning for him anyway, he would make sure he carried out his plans for the both of them.

Having seen enough, he left the scene to plan his reign of terror.

***

"How the hell did this happen?" Garrett screamed at the officer in charge. "You were supposed to be watching them!"

The officers who were assigned to watch the Unger's were lured to the next street over by what they thought was rapid gunfire, only to discover it was only high grade fireworks thrown on someone's porch. By the time they had calmed the homeowner and returned to their post, the house was fully involved and there was nothing they could do. Even though the occupants were long dead, the officers could still hear their screams in their heads; screams that would amplify their nightmares for a long time to come.

Garrett was beside himself. He paced the sidewalk while the fire department worked desperately to contain the fire. Someone had deliberately set it; trapping everyone inside, including Patricia Unger and her son. Both doors, front and back, had been barricaded from the outside preventing anyone from escaping. Patricia, her son and the cousins she was staying with, were dead. Garrett couldn't believe this was happening. Nate clasped his shoulder trying to bring some comfort into a situation that would have none. They both now understood what they were up against and they both understood what they had to do.

***

Dressed in black, Jason Unger slipped around the side of Garrett's house, staying close to the walls to avoid the security cameras. It wasn't hard finding out where the D.A. lived. All he had to do was follow the man home.

Once Garrett lowered his garage door, Jason left his car to explore the grounds. He wanted to make sure he knew every nook and cranny of the place for when he was ready to implement his attack. He didn't want to leave anything to chance.

He would take his enemies down one at a time. When he was finished with the D.A. he would move on to his former attorney. They both had to pay for trying to put him away. And the way he figured it, he was already on the hook for the deaths of his wife and son, so he would make damn sure if he went down, he had taken the two along with him.

After gathering all the information he needed, Jason slipped back to his car and drove away. It was time to put his revenge in motion.

Chapter 29

It was dark when Queen parked across the street from Allison's. She had been driving around for hours crying. She had lost the only friend who ever really cared about her. Maybe it was her own fault by being so possessive of Myka, but she wanted to keep Myka safe from the things that had happened to her.

Needing a friend to talk to and not her girls from her neighborhood, she decided to pay Allison a visit. But before she could leave her car to mount the stairs to her apartment, she spotted Allison pulling out of her parking spot.

Queen sighed. Allison didn't have time for her either. But instead of going home, she decided to follower her. She was curious to see where she was headed. As Allison drove farther from the city and into what she referred to as the rich people's hood, Queen became more curious. Who did Allison know in this part of town. The last time they were together, she hinted that she had a new man, but never gave up his name.

Forgetting her woes for a minute, Queen finally smiled. Maybe Allison was going to meet her new dude. And if so, this was her chance to see who he was. She followed Allison through neighborhoods she could only dream about living. Finally turning onto a circular drive, Queen stopped her car on the street and watched Allison exit her car. She watched her push the bell at the beautiful home; waiting for someone to answer. When the door was finally pulled open, Queen's jaw dropped when Derrick Steele stepped into view. She was stunned to see him pull Allison into his arms to kiss her.

"Oh my gawd, Oh my gawd!" Queen couldn't believe what she was seeing. Allison was sleeping with Myka's man. Queen picked up her phone to call Myka, but remembered she was no longer Myka's friend. Tossing the phone into her purse, she put her car in gear and drove off. It was no longer her business. From now on, whatever happened to Myka would be her own fault.

Chapter 30

Derrick rolled off of Allison. He had so many irons in the fire he couldn't concentrate. It had been days since the last time he saw Myka and that self righteous asshole Pleasant, but he was still upset. He thought his earlier excursion would have calmed him down some but it hadn't done much for his rage against Garrett. Myka was spending too much time with him and from what he could see, she had fallen for the guy. This was not how this was supposed to go. Myka was supposed to be broken, not rewarded with a man who deemed himself better than he was.

He looked over at Allison. He had hoped her presence would make him feel better, but it hadn't. The high from screwing one of Myka's friends was just not there anymore. He didn't want *Allison* anymore. It was time he got rid of her.

"Get dressed. It's time for you to leave." Derrick bound from the bed heading for the shower.

"What do you mean leave? I thought I was staying the night," she whined. Something was off with Derrick and she noticed it the moment he pushed inside of her. He was rough, more than usual. Most of the time she could handle his pounding and hair pulling, but tonight it was

unbearable. She cried out several times before he finally
rolled off her.

"I'm going to have to pass on that," he told her.

"How can you pass on something this good?"
Allison asked him while running her fingers between her
thighs.

Derrick stopped in his tracks to turn to face her.
"Babe, it was good while it lasted, but I no longer require
your company. So get your things and be gone by the time I
get out of the shower. You're time with me is over. And
another thing, don't flatter yourself. You're no Myka
Ellis." With this parting shot, he continued on to the
bathroom.

Allison was furious. She couldn't understand why
he was throwing her out. She thought she was his new
woman. To add to her fury, her conscience spoke up. *You
know why he's throwing you out. Its Myka he wants and
always will.*

Myka wins again! She was so sick of that bitch. She
had everything: money, a thriving company and two men
vying for her attention.

Allison threw a pillow across the room towards
Derrick's bathroom. She was sick of Myka Ellis.

***

Stepping into the steaming shower, Derrick hoped Allison had the good sense to be gone when he returned to his bedroom. He threw that extra shot at her not being Myka, to get her moving along. No she wasn't Myka Ellis, and that was the problem.

Myka had continued to defy him by rebuffing his advances and now she was seeing Garrett Pleasant regularly. He didn't know when it happened, but he hated the man. Garrett had everything: money, prestige, and the ability to attract women like Myka. She reminded him of Garrett's girlfriend in law school. Kimber was sweet and sensitive, the kind of woman who usually shied away from the likes of him. He hadn't even wanted the woman, until Garrett confided that he loved her.

Derrick had been jealous of Garrett from the moment they met. Everything came easy to Garrett. It was as if the man were living a charmed life; as if he belonged to some sort of club that he could never be a part of, no matter how hard he tried. So when the opportunity came along to seduce his precious Kimber, Derrick took it and her.

Kimber hadn't been as hard to persuade as he thought. He soon found out why. She was nothing like what he or Garrett perceived her to be. Kimber was just another tramp pretending to be a good girl. Derrick discovered she had slept with half the campus back in her undergrad years. After discovering her deception, he had beaten her for it. Here he was thinking he was getting over on Garrett, when it was Kimber who had gotten over on the both of them. Derrick was enraged when he discovered the woman was nothing more than a cheap whore.

Turning off the water, he stepped from the shower; draping a towel around his lower half. Listening for movement, he padded back into his bedroom to find Allison gone. If she hadn't left, he would have given her the same treatment he gave Kimber.

Chapter 31

Nate stood in his office looking out over the darkened city. It was after hours with only a few people still working on his floor. He should have been over the moon at the news that the police had arrested Jamal Linden, but after witnessing the death of Patricia Unger and her young son, it was hardly time to celebrate.

He had gotten the call about Jamal while he and Garrett were at the scene watching the firemen extinguish the flames. Just as they had hoped, Linden logged into his account, giving them his whereabouts. The police immediately swarmed the hotel and arrested him.

He, in turn, called Cymone to give her the good news. Her money would be transferred into her account first thing in the morning. At least one good thing came out of this hellish day. Now on top of everything else, he may be Jason Unger's next target. He would retrieve his gun from its locked box as soon as he arrived home. There was no sense in taking a chance as long as the man was walking around free.

Nate turned at a knock on his door. Checking his watch, his brow furrowed. He wasn't expecting anyone. Instead of asking his visitor to come in, he moved to open the door himself. If it was Unger, he wanted a chance to engage him immediately.

He cautiously opened the door to Cymone. Nate smiled.

"I know you weren't expecting me, but I wanted to thank you in person for all you've done to get my money back, *and* to restore my dignity. I come, bearing gifts." She held up the two takeout bags she was carrying. They were from her favorite Chinese restaurant. "I hope you like Chinese."

Nate nodded. He was so surprised to see her, he had yet to utter a word. "Wow. I must say this is a pleasant surprise. Here let me take those. He took her packages and placed them on a nearby table. "Everything smells wonderful."

Before he could ask her what was in the bags, Cymone kissed him. First it was just a peck on the lips; then more passionately as she pulled him closer to her. Food forgotten Nate enclosed her in his arms as he took the lead. He had wanted to kiss her from the first time he saw her. Pulling her even closer, he explored ever inch of her mouth as he hungrily devoured her. Now that her case was solved, he could indulge in everything Cymone, and he planned to do that for the rest of the evening.

Chapter 32

"What do you mean pointers?"

All the color had drained from Myka's face. He couldn't be serious, but he was. Garrett wanted her to give him pointers on how to seduce a woman. Here was a handsome, intelligent, successful man sitting across from her. How could she give him pointers?

They were meeting in her conference room. It was early evening and everyone else in the office had left for the day. It was her idea to wait until the office was empty to work on the revisions for his novel, but she was quickly regretting this. She was comfortable with the arrangement until he asked for her help on a topic he should have been well versed in. Now all of a sudden the space seemed too quiet, and too intimate. Maybe meeting with him alone after dark wasn't such a good idea.

Garrett readily agreed to the afterhours meeting because he needed a distraction from Patricia Unger's death. He couldn't shake the guilt of not being able to keep her and her son Jamie safe from her husband. He needed a diversion, and working on his book with Myka seemed like the perfect solution. And after her reaction to his request, he was glad he came.

"You know, what makes a woman fall into a man's arms? And I'm talking about a real woman. Not these females who have no shame in thrusting their every asset in a man's face. I mean a lady that likes to be courted and pursued."

Garrett was enjoying her discomfort. Myka Ellis had erected a wall of concrete around herself and he fully understood why after learning of her involvement with Derrick Steele. But he wanted to prove to her he was the polar opposite of Derrick. Even if it meant taking a sledge hammer to that self erected wall of hers. He wanted his seduction of her to be swift. He wanted it to be so urgent that she didn't have time to ward it off. And if he could get her to participate in making it happen, even better.

Myka stood from her chair and walked across the room to a wall of windows to put some distance between them. All of a sudden she couldn't breathe. She had to give it to him; he was dedicated to this quest. After she made her suggestions he didn't tarry. He accepted the challenge and pressed forward immediately. She should have kept her big mouth shut. But then again, she had her own goal, and that was to make his book number one. And from his determination, he wanted this every bit as much as she did.

Pulling herself together, she turned towards him again. "Tell me about your dates."

"My dates?" He didn't expect her to recover quite so quickly and not with this topic.

"Yes your dates. What is a typical date for you?" Myka found she was interested and not just for the book either. Garrett rubbed his chin. Something Myka noticed he did when he was uncertain about something.

"Well, apart from drinks, usually it comes down to dinner or some event or function. And if the night goes well, back to her place for a night cap or more, if she's game." Garrett shrugged. Saying it out loud sounded lame to his own ears, not to mention the reaction from Myka.

Myka's jaw dropped. This man really didn't have a clue. "Garrett, where is the romance, the fire and passion? Where is the intrigue? Tell me this; when was your last relationship?

Garrett blinked. Now *he* was uncomfortable. "I'll answer your last question first. My last *real* relationship was a few years ago. And as for the fire—."

Myka held up her hand stopping him. "Stop, you don't have to go any further. If your last relationship was years ago, I'm willing to bet there was no fire or anything else, otherwise she would still be around. What have you been doing all of this time?"

He shrugged again. "Working."

His motives for not participating fully in a relationship were more self preservation than what he led her to believe. Sure his job was demanding and took up a lot of his time; but if he were honest with himself, he had been hesitant because of the incident with Derrick. But with Myka, he felt that would not be a problem.

Myka shook her head. A part from writing those steamy tidbits for his novel herself, she had her work cut out for her. She couldn't believe the man. As intelligent as he was, he knew nothing about love and affection. Yes, she was going to help him and make this the best novel Ellis Publications ever produced if it killed her.

She knew she was going to regret asking her next question, but she really wanted to know. "Garrett. In your sexual relationships, is there at least some form of something hinting at foreplay?" She sincerely hoped he wasn't a wham, bam thank you ma'am. And if he was, no wonder he was still a single man.

This time it was Garrett who was shocked. He never expected her to be bold enough to ask about his sex life.

And in answering the question, he much rather show her instead.

"Do you mean hugs, kisses…touching? Yeah, I do all of that." He grinned at her eye roll. "Well, I do accomplish that much thank you." Actually, he was very capable of providing much more than that, but for the right woman. He firmly believed emotions should play a big part in how a woman was treated in and out of bed.

Myka folded her arms with a smirk. "Ok Pleasant, here is the rundown. A woman likes to be caressed and not just touched or fondled. Held and not just hugged; and when it comes to kisses, they must, and I repeat must, be long, deep and heartfelt. You have got to make her feel it down to her toes. A woman needs to know she is genuinely wanted and not just wanted in the sack. And fire? That fire must spill over into every aspect of your relationship even when you're not physically in the same place." Myka was pretty satisfied with her advice, and was so caught up mentally patting herself on the back; she never saw what came next.

Without warning, Garrett crossed the room, pulled her into his arms and firmly planted his mouth on hers. When she parted her lips to protest, he expertly slipped his tongue inside her mouth, while drawing her closer to him.

When he felt no resistance, he kissed her long and deep; dueling with her tongue as she returned the kiss with the same vigor. Her arms had slipped around his neck drawing him even deeper. Garrett enjoyed the feel of her full breasts pressed against him, causing his body to become more deeply involved. After awhile, he couldn't tell if the moans originated from him or her. They could have gone on all night, if they hadn't needed to come up for air.

Garrett pulled away first, resting his forehead against hers. "Is that what you meant?" Myka could only nod. They both were trying to catch their breaths.

Wanting more of her, Garrett drew her into another kiss. This time he maneuvered her backwards, laying her back against the conference room table without breaking the kiss. Myka could feel his erection as he positioned himself between her legs. He had pushed her skirt up high around her thighs, exposing her black lace panties. Gathering her in his arms, he settled himself on top of her, while they indulged in another incredible kiss.

Myka didn't know this man, but she wanted him now. Pulling his shirt from his belted trousers, she attempted to undo the buttons only to become frustrated with the task. Feeling her pain, Garrett ripped it apart sending buttons flying everywhere. He quickly relieved himself of the offending item, by tossing it to the other side of the table.

With that layer gone, Myka slipped her hands underneath his undershirt, helping him to remove it too. While she unbuckled his belt, Garrett slid her panties down her legs and added them to the growing pile of clothes on the floor. He removed her blouse to kiss the tops of her overflowing breasts, encased in her matching black bra.

After sending the last bit of clothing flying, Garrett planted his mouth on a swollen breast as Myka writhed beneath him. The more she moved and moaned the more aroused he became. His body screamed for relief, but he wanted to show her what he knew about passion. He wanted to take his time to seduce her properly.

He took his time by leaving a slow, hot trail of kisses down to the apex of her legs, where he paused to kiss her intimately. Myka came unglued with the erotic sensations that engulfed her. She thought she would die from his mouth's work. She briefly concluded that his name should be Pleasure with what he was doing to her.

When she thought she couldn't take anymore, he joined them with one swift thrust, sending her completely over the edge. Myka screamed with the sensation. Garrett held back to not only let her body adjust to him, but to also give himself time to adjust to her. Her walls were wrapped around him so tight, if he wasn't careful, he would lose his mind.

When he was sure he was in control again, he thrust slowly at first, not wanting to hurt her. But after she grabbed his hips urging him on, he picked up the tempo, moving faster with every plunge, until they both begged for release. Myka came with the force of a small tornado, with vibrations ricocheting throughout her body. Garrett soon followed with a powerful release of his own. He rolled off of her to drop into the nearest chair. He didn't think he would ever catch his breath.

***

While the two were recovering, unbeknownst to them, someone had witnessed the entire act and wasn't pleased.

Chapter 33

"Allison?"

Cymone's eyes narrowed at what Nate just shared with her. From his description of the woman he described, it *was* Allison. This surprised her, because if she had to choose the woman to stab Myka in the back, it would have been Queen Bitch.

They were sitting on a blanket on the floor eating the food she'd brought. Nate found it tucked in a closet in his office and had spread it out before they made love. He wanted their first time to be in his bed, but once their lips met, he found it impossible not to take the next step then and there.

In her mind, Cymone turned over everything he told her, but was finding it hard to swallow. She never viewed Allison as any sort of threat. In fact, out of the four of them she was the most reliable. She was always agreeable with whatever the group came up with; never balking at any of their plans. She was so agreeable, Cymone nicknamed her Miss Go Along. She would have to think more on this revelation. But still, Nate had no reason to lie about seeing her all cozy with Derrick. If this was true, had she been sleeping with him all along, even when he and Myka were together? She didn't know the answers to those questions, but in the meantime, Allison St. James needed to be watched.

After Nate brought up the subject of Allison, Cymone explained Allison's friendship with her and Myka. She also told him about Queen and how Myka had to cut ties with her over her clinginess among other things. Nate shared his history pertaining to both Garrett and Derrick. He explained the strain between them, after Garrett caught Derrick with his girlfriend in law school.

Nate could tell she was having a difficult time accepting what he'd told her about her friend. He had almost forgotten about the woman, until he saw her kissing Derrick when they both thought no one was looking.

He was leaving a hearing when he spotted the two duck into an empty courtroom. Curious, he followed where he witnessed them all but having sex right then. Was Derrick the reason why Allison was so interested in his and Garrett's conversation that night at the bar? He wondered if Garrett knew Derrick was Myka's ex. And would this revelation halt Garrett's interest in Myka? He hoped not.

Cymone, finished with her food, stood to put her clothes back on. She smiled down at Nate who was busy scraping the last of the noodles from the carton. The man had worked up quite an appetite.

"Leaving so soon?" He asked.

She bent down to kiss him. "Yes. I have an early meeting in the morning that I need to finish preparing for." She kissed him again.

"Wait a minute and I'll walk you down." He didn't want her leaving the building alone. It was after dark and most of the time that portion of the street was deserted. He wanted to make sure she was safe in her car.

After making sure Cymone was secure and on her way home, Nate came back upstairs to clean up. His day may have had a rough start, but it definitely ended on a high note.

He smiled. Cymone Davis was about to be bombarded with attention and this time the right kind.

Chapter 34

"I've been calling your cell phone all morning."

Myka was startled at the closeness of Derrick's voice. He was at her side before she realized it. She was headed out the building to meet Garrett for lunch.

Derrick had waited in the lobby for her to come downstairs. He instructed Tessa to call him the moment she knew when Myka would be taking lunch. Even though he knew her interests lied with Garrett, he wasn't about to let up on steering her back in his direction.

She stopped long enough to rebuff him—again. "Derrick I am not having lunch with you now or ever again. We're over. Why can't you accept that? I don't want anything else to do with you, so if you please…" She waited for him to let her pass. Frustrated, she wanted to scream. What was it going to take for his ego to agree that they were done? She shook her head as she pushed through the doors.

Derrick watched her exit the building. He was not pleased. His jaw tightened at the reason she wouldn't take his calls or spend time with him—Garrett Pleasant. He would just have to make sure Garrett wouldn't be a problem. Garrett Pleasant was never a match for him when it came to women and he wasn't about to let him start now. Frustrated, Derrick took the elevator to Myka's floor. He needed to see Tessa.

***

Mark pressed himself against the wall as he strained to catch every word of Derrick and Tessa's conversation. He was about to leave for lunch when Derrick strolled in. He never liked the man and always thought Myka could have done better. Just because he had a law degree and plenty of money to throw around didn't necessarily make him the catch of the century.

Pulling her purse from a desk drawer, Tessa sighed. "She's gone already," she told Derrick before he could ask. She knew he was there for Myka and not her. He hadn't visited her since he learned Garrett Pleasant's interest in Myka.

"I know that," he snapped. "I just saw her get into Garrett's car. You were supposed to be keeping him occupied."

Derrick was angry. Myka wouldn't return any of his calls or accept any of the gifts he sent. She had each of them returned. He even sent the ring he had supposedly sent out to be sized. In truth, the ring was on loan, since he never intended to use it and still didn't. He just needed it to bait Myka. This time he had the jeweler to loan him one in her size, but it too was returned.

Tessa frowned. "I can't make the man want me," she snapped back. She had tried everything, but he wouldn't bite. She showed up at the coffee shop, the courthouse. She even tried cozying up to his friend Nate Morrison for help, but nothing. To her displeasure, like Derrick, Garrett Pleasant wanted Myka.

Derrick drew a hand down his face. He would have to come up with something else to get Myka away from Garrett. Obviously Tessa wasn't up to the task. But in the mean time...

Looking around the office, he asked, "Where is everybody?"

"We only had the regular staff here today. And I think Mark left for lunch already." Tessa was pouting. She couldn't capture Garrett's attention and Derrick was too busy trying to get Myka back to have time for her.

Noticing Tessa's disappointment, Derrick opened his arms. "Come here." He tried soothing her with his most seductive voice.

Tessa hesitated at first, but slowly moved forward to be engulfed in his outstretched arms. He pulled her into his embrace, kissing her deeply.

Wanting to see what was going on, Mark took a chance to peer around the corner just as Derrick's hand slid down Tessa's back to her backside. He watched him squeeze her bottom while grinding himself against her.

Mark was taken aback by this vulgar display. He had no idea how well Tessa knew Derrick, let alone intimately. Retreating to his position along the wall, he certainly didn't want either one of them to know he was there. He slowly shook his head. He didn't know who was more pathetic, Tessa or Derrick. He was glad Myka was with Garrett. Derrick turned out to be every bit of the scum he thought he was.

Mark closed his eyes. Now what was he going to do about Derrick's connection to Tessa. She needed rescuing from the likes of Derrick Steele, but was he up to the task? After witnessing her interaction with Derrick, he knew he should drop his interest in her, but it made him want her even more.

After a few minutes Derrick released Tessa and left; promising to call her later. After Tessa gathered her things and headed for the elevators, Mark stepped into the lobby from his hiding place. He couldn't believe what he'd just witnessed. And what was he going to do about it?

***

Mark wasn't the only one to observe Derrick and Tessa's exchange. Cameron caught what transpired between the two also.

He had just gotten off the elevator and was poised to enter Ellis Publications to visit his friend, when he spotted them. Stopped in his tracks, Cameron turned on his heels and got back on the elevator to his floor, too stunned to watch anymore. Now he understood what drove Tessa to do the things she did, and he was appalled. Out of all the men in the city she could have hooked up with, why did it have to be with Derrick Steele? Knowing everything there was to know about Tessa, Cameron knew for certain Derrick was not the man for her.

Getting off on his floor, he shook his head. The poor girl had deeper troubles than anyone could have ever imagined.

Chapter 35

The hairs on the back of Jason's neck stood out as
he turned to search for the source of the uneasy feeling. He
was standing outside of Garrett's house; hidden from the
street by the tall shrubbery that lined the exterior walkway.

He was watching him move around his customized
kitchen, presumably preparing his dinner. But at the same
time, he felt as if he were the one being watched. He peered
through the shrubbery at the neighboring houses and at a
lone car parked a few yards down the street. He didn't see
anyone, but felt the unease just the same. Taking just one
more peek at his target, he stepped through the bushes and
scampered across the lawn to follow the shadows casted by
the tree lined street to his car. Turning up the heat in the
car, Jason rubbed his hands together. After understanding
Garrett's routine, he had a plan, and would come back the
following night to execute it. It was time for Mr. D. A. to
pay.

***

Had Jason Unger turned to look behind him, he
would have caught sight of the person stalking him. The
stalker had stepped out of the shadows long enough to cross
the street and duck into a darkened area of a neighbor's

yard. Pulling a cell phone from a coat pocket, Jason Unger's pursuant placed an anonymous call to the police, concerning a peeping Tom in the neighborhood. The caller gave Jason's description and the car he was driving. Having accomplished the task for the night, the caller pocketed the untraceable phone and walked swiftly back to a stolen car. It was time to execute the master plan.

Chapter 36

Garrett woke up disoriented and coughing. Something was wrong but his mind couldn't quite register what. He tried focusing on the sound that seemed to be buzzing from his head. Trying harder, he realized the blaring noise was his home's smoke detectors going off. His house was on fire.

Forcing himself to roll over, he dragged himself to the edge of the bed and dropped onto to the floor, where he pulled himself by his elbows to a set of doors that led out to a side yard. Moving slowly he managed to open the ornate doors and crawl outside, just as several people appeared in his yard. Losing consciousness, Garret felt hands tugging on him, but was unable to comprehend what was going on. He finally blacked out.

***

"Garrett? Garrett? Can you hear me?" Nate was trying to get Garrett to open his eyes.   Garrett's eyes fluttered open, merely to close again. He tried focusing on Nate's voice. When he opened his eyes again, he attempted to sit up, only to be stopped by a severe pounding in his head.

"Whoa there buddy. You need to take it easy." Nate placed a hand on his shoulder to keep him from moving.

"Wha…what happened?" He asked from a throat that was raspy and raw. Garrett closed his eyes once more; trying to clear his mind.

Nate was relieved. "Man you're lucky to be alive. The fire chief says someone set your house on fire. They found accelerant all around the place." Nate found out about the fire from one of Garrett's neighbors, who helped pull him away from the burning house. The man was a client of Nate's and knew he and Garrett were friends.

Still trying to fight off the headache, Garrett carefully cleared his throat. "My head. Where am I?" He clenched his teeth hoping the pounding would stop.

"You're at Metro Regional. The doctor said you inhaled quite a bit of smoke, but you'll live. And as for your head…one of the nurses just came in to give you something for that. You should feel some relief soon. I'm just glad you're still here to complain."

"No Thanks to Jason Unger, I'm sure." Garrett leaned over to one side to cough.

"Well yeah, he was the first person to pop in my mind too. I have no doubt the man tried to kill you. Your

office has every available officer looking for the scumbag."
If he had any doubt before, Nate now knew Unger's
vendetta was real. He just hoped they found him before he
did more damage. He had already killed his wife and child
and now he was after Garrett.

"Could you do me a favor?"

"Anything."

"Find Myka Ellis for me and make sure she's safe.
If that idiot finds out he didn't succeed at killing me, he
may take it out on those close to me. Myka and I have
gotten closer in the last few weeks." Garrett coughed again.
He wanted to do it himself but he felt terrible. There was no
way he was going to be able to do anything tonight.

"You got it."

Nate pulled his phone from his pocket to call
Cymone. He didn't have Myka's number, but knew
Cymone would get him in touch with her. And speaking of
Cymone. If that lunatic was going after Garrett, he could be
certain that he was next. That meant he needed to protect
Cymone as well. And taking Cymone's stubbornness into
account, he anticipated having a fight on his hands. He was
just going to have to find a way to convince her it was for
her own good.

***

Garrett opened his eyes when he felt someone touch his hand. After Nate left, a nurse had given him a sedative which put him out immediately. When he turned his head, he found Myka smiling down at him.

"There you are. I thought you would never wake up. They must have you on some really good stuff." She wore a smile, even though she didn't feel it. When Nate called with the news of what happened, she nearly panicked. Garrett could have been killed. Nate didn't tell her why or how the fire started; he left that up to Garrett. He had his own problem with convincing Cymone to take precautions.

Garrett smiled. "I'm happy to see your smiling face." And he meant it. His last thought before passing out, was that he would never see her again.

"What time is it…how long have you been here?" He felt as if he had been asleep for days.

As if reading his mind she answered him. "It's early evening. You've been asleep for quite some time. I came as soon as Nate called me this morning and that was before the sun had come up."

She smiled again and this time it was genuine. She had been right by his side the entire day, only leaving once to call the office to cancel her appointments. Nate had been gracious enough to bring her food and Cymone had come along with him. Even though she said they weren't an item, Myka could tell both she and Nate were very much into each other.

Garrett cleared his still raw throat. "Did Nate tell you anything about the fire?" Myka shook her head. Garrett cleared his throat again. "We believe it was intentionally set."

Myka gasped. "What do you mean intentionally?"

"Nate and I were working on this case where this guy tried to kill his wife and kid. And to make a long story short, he vowed to get even with us if he ever got out. Well he's out, and has finished the job on his family, by setting the house they were staying in on fire, killing everyone inside.

"What are you going to do? And Nate's in danger too?" Myka was beside herself. She thought this was an accident not an attempt at murder.

"The police are looking for the guy and yes Nate is probably in danger too. But don't worry, we will catch this guy." He paused before bringing up his next topic. "Myka, you may also be in danger, you and Cymone both, because of your connection to me and Nate. We don't know where this guy's head is, but we need to keep you both safe." He hated to scare her, but this was no game. Jason Unger was playing for keeps and they had to play just as hard to stay alive.

"From what I understand your house was destroyed; where are you going to live?" She didn't want to think about the danger they may all be in right now. She was more worried about him.

Garrett shrugged. "I'm sure that won't be a problem. I can stay in a hotel and decide what to do from there."

Myka shook her head. "No you won't. You are going to move in with me. Why pay for some cold, impersonal room when you can be with…" Myka trailed off. What was she going to say; someone who loved him? "Someone you know and I won't charge you by the night. How about that?" She smiled; trying to deflect what she was really feeling. Feelings that she herself didn't understand. They hadn't known each other that long, but still.

Garrett caught her pause, but chose not to dwell on it. He would let it rest for now. He did agree to move in with her until things were settled. He thought this was an excellent idea. That way he could keep an eye on her and keep her safe. Jason Unger would have to go through him to get to Myka.

Chapter 37

Derrick's jaw tightened with renewed anger as he listened to Janice Steele go on and on about what *she* wanted. What about what *he* wanted? Everything that he managed to touch these days seemed to fail and it all led back to Myka.

Now here he was listening to his mother make demands that he didn't have time to be bothered with. He had bigger issues to settle. He was becoming very weary of his mother and he told her so. She just brushed his complaints off and chalked it up to him being over worked.

Derrick may have been overloaded, but it wasn't from work. With uncompleted projects in the works and with his mother nagging him constantly, he did have many irons in the fire. It was time he completed a couple of those tasks, before he lost his control.

Sometimes he envied his father. Instead of allowing his wife to knuckle him down to her will, he just drank himself to death. No. He knew when he finally had enough of his mother, he would put a stop to her constant pressure and control once and for all. He just hadn't decided on the method.

Janice had changed gears and was now pressuring him to have dinner with her to discuss her trip. After bearing his mother's voice for as long as he could stand it, he cut her off in mid sentence; telling her he would get back to her and hung up. He didn't understand why she couldn't go out on her own or with a group of her friends. Before his sister moved away, she kept their mother, somewhat distracted, with criticisms of the men Blake chose. But having had enough of Janice, she had the good sense to tuck tail and run. She just packed up her things one day and left the country with some rich prince she met at one of her elaborate social events.

Derrick couldn't understand why Janice insisted on insinuating herself into every aspect of his life. He thought by giving her anything she wanted, would get her off his back, but it hadn't. If anything, she dug herself in deeper. He wished she would find a man who could tolerate her and leave town too.

Fingering his cell phone, he picked it up again to punch in a single programmed number. He needed sexual release to take away the tension that had built up over the past few days. A session of bodies in motion always did the trick, and he needed it now.

Chapter 38

It had taken a lot to convince Cymone to move in with him until Unger was caught, but she did. Nate hated to do it, but after he explained what happened to Patricia Unger and her baby, he knew she would stop resisting. He even persuaded her to work from his house instead of going in to the office. He would never forgive himself if she were hurt because of him.

He moved Cymone into his home the day after Garrett's incident. He would have suggested that Myka join the party, if Garrett had stayed another day in the hospital as the doctors suggested. But once his mind was made up, they had to concede with the promise that he would take it easy for the next several days. Nate was glad to hear he was moving in with Myka. That way he could keep her safe.

Nate watched Cymone do a little dance while she made them dinner. Over the past couple of days, he learned that she was an excellent cook. Being a bachelor, he ate out more than he cared to admit and was grateful for the home cooked meals.

"Have you talked to Myka today," he asked, while trying to sneak a taste from her simmering dish. Cymone playfully slapped his hand.

"Yes." She stuck a finger in the pot to taste for herself. "Garrett has placed himself on indefinite leave and has been going into the office with her while they work to launch his book."

Nate's focus was drawn from the pot to what Cymone was saying. "Book? What book?"

Cymone's eyes widened. *Oops. Did I say something I wasn't supposed to?* Realizing she may have made a mistake in mentioning it, she tried distracting him with a spoonful of stew.

Accepting the stew, but not the ploy, Nate asked again. "Are you going to tell me about this book or not?" He was curious. Garrett never mentioned anything about a book to him.

She sighed. It was out of the bag now. She would have to beg for Myka's forgiveness later. "Garrett has written a crime novel and Myka's publishing it. But you can't let them know I told you. If Garrett hasn't mentioned it, maybe he wanted it to be a surprise." She hoped that was the case or they both were going to kill her.

Nate grinned. "Good for him. I'm sure he has much material to draw from." He was truly glad for his friend. He remembered years ago, Garrett mentioned writing a book. He was happy that he finally got to it.

"Is there any word on that maniac that tried to make Garrett a crispy critter?" Cymone asked.

"So far, all we have is a 911 call about a peeping Tom fitting Unger's description seen wandering Garrett's neighborhood. That, with the license plate of the car he was driving, puts him there. So it stands to reason he was the one to torch Garrett's home. But other than that, no word. He hasn't been seen anywhere. We had a tip that he was holed up in a motel on the outskirts of town, but when the police got there, he was gone. The photo they showed the clerk puts him there without a doubt. Now we just need to lay eyes on him."

"Well, I for one will be glad when that fool is caught." Cymone shook her head. There were too many evil people running around town. With all of this happening on the heels of the arrest of the former mayor and police chief, the city was turning into something unrecognizable.

Nate was about to second that when his phone rang. Reaching for the cordless, he answered. Cymone watched his demeanor change from jovial to concerned. She wondered what had happened now. Saying only a few words to the caller, Nate hung up.

"What's wrong?" Cymone turned off the stove to give her full attention to Nate. Something wasn't right.

Nate released a slow and steady breath. "Jamal somehow escaped federal custody. There was a big commotion in court this morning and in the midst of the melee he slipped away without notice."

Cymone threw up her hands. "So now we have two lunatics on the loose? What the hell is going on in this city?"

Nate shrugged. "The marshals are looking for him. He shouldn't be able to get far without any money. Then again, he has ways of supporting his needs." Nate felt like Cymone. What was happening to their city?

Chapter 39

Janice Steele dropped her teacup in horror when she pushed open the door to her son's bedroom. The sight of Derrick, and the woman he was in bed with, was more than she bargained for.

Assuming he wasn't home after not answering the doorbell, Janice used her key to let herself into Derrick's house. She made herself at home, by brewing a pot of tea while she waited for him to return. She knew Derrick thought he had put her off, by not agreeing to take her to dinner, but she was determined to have her way. The whole point of sharing a meal was to discuss the details of her upcoming trip to Las Vegas. She wanted money and plenty of it. Janice planned to spend a week there shopping, seeing some shows and yes gambling. Although Derrick was being contrary now, she didn't foresee any resistance. He never denied her before, so she didn't understand why he just didn't agree to have dinner and get it over with. And when he came home, to find her lounging about uninvited, oh well, he would get over it.

Janice was what her late husband called a ball-breaker. The kind of woman who refused to let a man be a man. Paul Steele tried taming his wife early on in their marriage, only to fail miserably. In Janice's eyes, Paul never made enough money no matter how hard he worked or how much money he made. Nothing was ever good enough. In the beginning, he would work to give her whatever she wanted, but soon realized it was hopeless, because she would never be satisfied. After awhile, he just stopped trying to please her; only earning enough to keep a roof over the family's heads and a bottle in his hand. Her acid tongue and selfish ways soon sent him to an early grave via a whiskey bottle.

Paul drank nearly every day of his existence married to Janice. Once, one of his friends asked him why he didn't just leave her. He stated that Janice was like the devil; once she claimed your soul, you could never untie yourself from her. And with the only escape being death, he was correct. Paul Jermaine Steele died at the age of forty five, clutching his favorite bottle of hooch.

Since the death of her husband, Janice quite frankly demanded that Derrick do what Paul refused; take care of her every need. His only reprieve was when he moved out and attended college. But once he passed the bar and moved back to Metro City, she required him to be at her every beck and call. More so when he was with Myka, whom she disliked instantly.

Myka was the only woman who piqued any real interest from Derrick. Myka's presence in her son's life meant less attention on her.

Not understanding the dynamics of her son's relationship with Myka, Janice assumed Derrick's time and most importantly, money, was being funneled away from her. She had to put a stop to it. There was no way she was giving up her meal ticket under any circumstances. Who would take care of her if Derrick married? It never occurred to her once to get a job and take care of herself. As far as Janice was concerned, as long as Derrick was around to pamper her, why should she?

After brewing her favorite oolong tea, Janice had taken her cup to Derrick's bedroom to tidy up a bit. He never made his bed and always had clothes thrown all over the floor. She would make everything nice and neat by the time he made it home. She would even draw him a bath if he liked. It was the least she could do. Unlike her husband, she doted on her son, because he had the good sense to make something of himself and not drown in the bottom of a whiskey bottle. Derrick was her pride and joy, her one true accomplishment in the world.

As she neared the partially closed door, she heard the sounds of what her late husband used to call furniture moving. Those sounds meant Derrick was already home and had a woman in his bed. Janice's back became ramrod straight. She hoped it wasn't that Myka. And if it was, she would get rid of her once and for all.

Thinking she was about to interrupt Derrick with the woman she despised the most, Janice pushed the door open to find not Myka, but her niece, her sister's daughter Tessa, on all fours joined with her son's pounding body. She would have fallen if she hadn't caught the door jamb on the way down. Although she was unable to make a sound, Janice thought the muffled thud of the cup hitting the plush carpeted floor, would have made them stop.

Derrick, hearing the sound, turned his attention towards his mother standing in the doorway. But instead of stopping his sexual onslaught of his first cousin, he sneered at her, as he continued to grind away inside an oblivious Tessa. So caught up in the multiple orgasms she was experiencing, Tessa never saw her aunt enter the room

Gathering herself, Janice fled down the hallway, grabbing her coat and purse as she ran for the front door. Once she reached her late model E-Class Mercedes—another one of her demands from her son—she threw up in the grass. Closing her eyes, she wiped her mouth with the back of her hand. Janice had to lean on the car a moment before she could get her mind to cooperate with her body.

It took her several tries at pulling the driver's side door open, before she realized she hadn't disengaged the lock. Once inside, she willed herself to calm down in order to start the car. Janice didn't bother with the seatbelt; she had to get out of there. Finally shifting the car in drive, she gunned it around the circular drive unto the street. She didn't stop until she pulled into her own driveway; grateful her mind wouldn't allow her to continue to register what she'd seen while she was driving. And mercifully, she was able to let herself inside her home before she broke down.

Janice slid to the floor and cried. Wondering what kind of monster had she given birth to.

***

Derrick stood looking out his bedroom window while Tessa took a shower. After his mother left, he had taken her two more times before he was satisfied. His lips lifted in satisfaction at the horror-struck expression he witnessed on his Janice's face. It didn't bother him one bit that she now knew he and Tessa were lovers. In fact, he felt vindicated after all of her demands. He laughed out loud when he thought of how he came to have Tessa in his bed in the first place. The ink had barely dried on his home's closing documents before Janice was pushing for his cousin to come live with him.

***

Derrick started sleeping with Tessa right after he landed the partnership with his law firm. To celebrate his accomplishments, he bought the house of his dreams and couldn't wait to show his mother one more thing that his father couldn't achieve.

But instead of her being happy for him, she thought he was now in the perfect position to help the family more. Apart from her own financial demands, she insisted that her sister's daughter move in with him, until she found a job and a place of her own. Tessa had just finished college and needed a place to stay. It hadn't gotten past him that not one time did Janice suggest the girl come live with her. She protested her home was too small and she needed her space. And since he had such an enormous house, Tessa would fit right in.

Derrick was furious. It didn't matter that he hadn't seen his cousin in years and knew nothing of her; or that he wanted to enjoy his new home alone, before opening it up to guests. He asked why Tessa couldn't just go back home to her mother's. But Janice reminded him of her sister's strict religious fanaticism, making it impossible for Tessa to live there in peace with his Aunt Iris's hellfire lifestyle. So as always, what mother wanted, mother got.

Derrick was still pouting when Tessa arrived on his doorstep. He hadn't recognized her at first. The girl he remembered was skinny and unattractive, but the woman who appeared at his door wasn't anything like what he remembered. He was actually taken aback at how attractive she was. The woman who stood before him was curvy, busty and beautiful. At least she was worth looking at he thought as he showed her to her room. He gave her a suite on the other side of the house, as not to disturb him. With any luck he wouldn't have to see the girl at all.

After helping her settle in, he went back to his home office to get some work done. After working several hours without eating, he ventured to the kitchen for some food. But instead of stopping to raid the fridge for his late night meal, he found himself drawn to Tessa's room. He told himself he would just check on her one last time to see if she had everything she needed.

Derrick followed music to the other side of the house to find the guest room's door ajar. Curious, he peered inside to find a very naked and very enticing Tessa, drying her hair in front of the room's full length mirror. After catching movement in the mirror's reflection, she noticed him watching. Derrick fully expected her to cover herself or at the very least rush to close the door. Tessa did neither.

Wide-eyed, Tessa continued to stare back at him even after he entered the room and closed the door behind him. Derrick convinced himself her silence was a sign that she wanted him just as much as he wanted her. And if she didn't, he would just have to persuade her otherwise. From that moment on, he and Tessa had an unspoken agreement and had been enjoying each other ever since.

Derrick grinned as he was pretty sure this was not what his mother had in mind when she told him to take care of his cousin. Yes, Janice had no one to blame but herself for what happened between him and Tessa.

Derrick's smile soon turned into fury. He equally faulted her for his loss of control over Myka. If it hadn't been for her demands and her need for power over his life, Myka would still be under his thumb and not playing house with Garrett Pleasant.

But it didn't matter. He was going to have Myka back one way or another. And after today, his mother would never interfere again. He was certain of that.

Derrick turned to kiss Tessa when she joined him at the window. They were both still naked. After thinking about his mother walking in on them, his smile returned with a growing erection. Not wanting it to go to waste, he swept Tess off her feet and carried her back to bed.

Chapter 40

Myka smiled as she rode the elevator down to the lobby. It was her turn to supply lunch for her and Garrett. Since Garrett's near death experience, he had been working out of her office while he was recovering. Although he would have been safe from Jason Unger in his office near the courthouse, he wasn't so sure about Myka. He still believed Unger would try and target her if he couldn't get to him, so he made it a point to stick to her as much as possible.

But today Garrett needed to retrieve files for an upcoming trial and had taken a taxi to his office. He knew Myka would be safe for the few minutes that he planned to be gone. In the meantime, Myka took this opportunity to venture out to pick up their lunch instead of having it delivered. It was a beautiful day and she wanted to feel the sun on her face. It had been hidden for nearly a week during the winter storm that brought them several inches of snow.

Every citizen in Metro City must have had the same idea as there were many packed along the busy sidewalks. Some of the eateries had several diners who chose to take their meals on their patios in order to take advantage of the warming sun. It was clear that most people had experienced cabin fever and were anxious to soak up the rare rays before the next snow storm that was due in a couple of days.

Myka had picked up her called-in order, and was weaving her way through the crowd back to the office when a severe pain shot through her left side. The pain was so great she dropped the bag she was carrying, sending food all over the sidewalk. Myka cried out as another sharp sting struck her. Her scream drew the attention of several people around her as she fell to the ground, with blood pouring from her side. One of the people among the growing spectators immediately identified himself as a doctor and shouted for someone to call 911. He quickly knelt to tend to Myka.

Springing into action, Dr. Jon Payne hurriedly accessed her injury and determined she had been stabbed. Scrutinizing the faces in the crowd, he searched for who might have done this. Holding Myka's' hand he asked her name and a few more questions to make sure she was alert. Satisfied that she was still with him, he removed his coat and pressed it to her wounds while he patiently waited for the ambulance to arrive.

Just as the EMTs pulled to a stop at the curb, Garrett pushed his way through the crowd of onlookers. He had arrived back at Myka's office to find that she had walked to a nearby eatery. Concerned, he came looking for her. Once he laid eyes on Myka lying on the sidewalk his concern was kicked up to panic.

"Myka! Myka?" Garrett was distraught at finding her there. He quickly knelt down beside her, turning her face towards him. He had to be sure that she was alive.

Dr. Payne, recognizing Garrett from the news, spoke to him. Mr. Pleasant, I'm Dr. Payne. She's going to be ok. I've accessed her condition…" Looking around them again, he thought he should keep her condition to himself until Myka was loaded into the ambulance.

Garrett, picking up on the doctor's meaning, gave him a quick nod. They would speak on this later, but for now, he was just grateful she was alive.

Garrett talked to Myka, reassuring her that he was right there and would not be going anywhere. She was calm but understandably frightened as she was lifted and placed into the ambulance. Garrett and Jon Payne climbed in after her.

"You want to tell me what's going on?" Garrett asked Dr. Payne while he soothingly smoothed back

Myka's hair. She had closed her eyes and was breathing oxygen due to a panic attack. More pain had ripped through her when the EMTs were lifting her onto the gurney.

Dr. Payne nodded his head. "She's been stabbed, and from the looks of it more than once. I happened to be walking past her when she dropped to the ground in pain."

"Could you see who might have done this?" Dr. Payne shook his head.

Garrett had to ask but he already knew. It was Jason Unger. He stabbed Myka. He could have kicked himself for leaving her alone. He should have told her he would bring them lunch, but he had no idea she would leave the office instead of their routine of having it delivered. He knew Myka just wanted to feel like a normal person again and not like she was constantly under house arrest. She stated earlier that she wanted to take advantage of the sunny day, but he thought she would at least wait until he returned. Garrett felt guilty. It was because of him that she was lying on a gurney speeding towards a hospital. And even though the doctor assured him that she would recover, he would never forgive himself.

***

Nate found Garrett on the phone, pacing the corridor of Metro Regional's ER. He was having a heated exchange with someone, and from his set jaw, the conversation wasn't getting any better. Ending the call, Garrett greeted his friend.

"How is she," Nate asked.

"She's in surgery. The doctor who was on the scene, told me she may lose a kidney, but she will recover…How could this happen?" Garrett shook his head as he pressed his fingers to his temples in frustration. He felt a migraine coming on. "What are the police saying?"

Garrett called Nate the moment they arrived at the hospital. He needed for him to make his way to the scene and see what he could find out.

It was Nate's turn to shake his head. "The police have interviewed everyone who stuck around, but no one saw anything. They were all either heading to lunch or back to work. The one thing they agreed upon was Myka's outcry and her dropping to the ground. Other than that, nothing." They both knew who was responsible and they didn't like it.

"What are the police saying about Unger?" Nate asked. He didn't need a psychic to know Unger's MIA status was what had Garrett in an uproar on the phone.

"I talked to Eric Valero, and they still don't know where he is and haven't known, since he was released from jail. It's like the man is a ghost. He does his dirt and no one sees him coming or going."

Just then, Dr. Payne pushed through the doors leading to the emergency surgery wing.

"Mr. Pleasant—"

"Garrett please, how is she?"

"She had some blood loss and once we got inside we discovered the blade had only nicked the kidney, so we were able to save it. All in all she is a very lucky young lady. She's in recovery now and should mend nicely."

Both Garrett and Nate released the tense breath they were holding. Myka was going to be ok. Dr. Payne shook hands with Garrett before returning to see about his patient.

"That's great news," Nate was saying. "Have you contacted her family?"

Garrett nodded. "Her cousin KT will be here shortly. She was out of town when I called her and is in the air as we speak. She was the only one on her emergency call list. If Myka has any other family, I don't know who that is. For some reason she doesn't like to talk about family, so I've adhered to her wishes." Garrett shrugged. "Did you tell Cymone?"

"Yes, a patrolman is bringing her."

As if on cue, Cymone rushed towards them. "How is she?"

Chapter 41

Janice Steele rode the elevator up to Ellis Publications. She was there to take her niece Tessa to lunch. She hadn't seen her, or Derrick for that matter, since the day she found them in bed together. Janice was appalled at Derrick's behavior, but even more so of her niece's. Although she didn't have to guess as to who instigated the abomination, she knew this was all Derrick's doing, by the way he greeted her that day. But still, if Tessa had kept her panties pulled up, none of this would be happening.

Janice tried to quiet that small voice in her head that knew who was really the sole blame. Deep down, she knew her son was out of control in his teens. Back then, Derrick was just a *little* troubled and would grow out of it—at least that was what she told herself. If she were honest, she would admit to seeing signs of his perverse behavior years before, yet she chose to ignore it. Derrick always had a mean streak as a child, but she chalked it up to her husband's emotional abandonment of the family. Paul never had time for the boy and pushed the responsibility of raising Derrick and his sister Blake all on her.

When Derrick was in high school, she watched him mistreat the girls he dated. If he didn't get his way with them, he would abruptly drop them and move on to a more willing victim. That is, if they were lucky. Once she overheard him bullying a girl into agreeing to have sex with him. The girl didn't want to, but it was Derrick and he always had his way regardless of any resistance. And instead of putting a stop to his brutish behavior, she pretended it wasn't a big deal. After all, boys will be boys.

There was one incident during his senior year, where a father of one of the girls he was dating came to the house. The man claimed Derrick had tried forcing himself on his daughter. When Derrick was confronted about the incident, he coolly denied it ever happened and all but called the girl a liar. Days later, she told her parents that she made it all up, because Derrick dumped her. Janice knew in her heart of hearts that Derrick did everything the girl said he had. She didn't have to wonder what made her change her story. She knew Derrick had changed it for her.

As for Tessa, there was no doubt in her mind that Derrick coerced her into the sickening relationship, but she saw her as the key to making it stop. Janice knew it was impossible to talk to her son, even if she wanted to. She had no intentions of confronting him about the matter. Derrick made known his position when he gleefully sneered at her when she discovered them.

Getting off the elevator, Janice took a moment to steady her nerves. The mere thought of that ugly scene gave her an upset stomach. But after today, she knew she could put it behind her as if it never happened. It would be an unpleasant chapter in their family history that would never see the light of day. She thought about calling her sister to tell her what she'd learned, but quickly thought better of that idea. If Derrick ever got wind of the disclosure, he would cut her off for sure.

Tessa looked up at the swoosh of the door opening with a smiled.

"Auntie!"

***

Tessa was still shaking when she tried inserting the key into the lock of her apartment door. Not able to manage her coordination at the moment, she rested her head on the cool wooden surface, trying to calm herself.

Janice had taken Tessa to one of her favorite fancy restaurants for lunch, where they were led to a private dining room, because she wanted to 'catch up' without being interrupted by the noise of the other diners. Tessa was happy when she sat down to dine with her aunt. It had been awhile since they had talked. Janice prolonged the rouse, by chatting away about her many travels, Tessa's job, and Janice's sister, whom Tessa hadn't spoken to in some time. For Tessa, things were going great until Janice mentioned Derrick.

Janice's whole countenance changed when the subject of her cousin was brought up. Tessa never saw it coming. Out of all the subjects her aunt could have discussed, sleeping with Derrick never made the list. All the blood had drained from Tessa's face once Janice revealed how she discovered they were sleeping together. She felt faint upon hearing her describe walking in on them and how Derrick received her. Her aunt knew and soon the whole world would know, including her mother. Tessa was mortified.

After Janice set off her little bomb, she dropped the loving aunt act and curtly told Tessa to stop the shameful, deplorable act immediately and get herself some help. She all but crucified her for her participation in the sexual escapades with her cousin; her darling son. Janice blamed her for the whole mess; calling her despicable trash, who would open her legs for anyone, even her own kin.

After having her say, Tessa watched Janice cut into her steak as if they had just discussed plans for a party.

Lunch was over for her. But instead of leaving, she had to endure Janice's smug satisfaction while she waited for the end of the meal to be sanctioned by her aunt. With her task completed, Janice was able to enjoy her meal whereas Tessa wanted to vomit into hers. So many emotions overcame her as she sat in stark silence. What would happen if this ever got out? She would be ruined.

Tessa left the restaurant on unsteady legs. Her world had collapsed and all she wanted to do was get home. But after trying to get into her aunt's car, to which she had ridden in, to the restaurant, Janice wouldn't hear of it. As far as she was concerned, her work was done. She had the hostess to call Tessa a taxi.

When the driver turned onto her street, Tessa felt as if she could breathe a little. She couldn't understand why her aunt attacked her so viciously. She wondered if she tore into Derrick the same way. Tessa doubted it. Not the way Janice depended on him. She began to doubt if she said anything to him at all. What was she supposed to do now? One thing was for certain; she couldn't go back to work; not today; maybe not ever.

Climbing out of the taxi, Tessa stood on the sidewalk as it pulled away. Deciding not to enter her building just yet, she crossed the street to the neighborhood store. Her mind was bombarded with thoughts and she needed something to drown out the horror of it all. After making her purchases, she made her way back to her building; grateful she had the elevator to herself, as she rode it to her floor.

Tessa pushed herself away from the door. This time when she used her key, it slid into the lock without difficulty. Dropping her keys and purse to the floor the moment the door closed, she rushed straight to her kitchen for a glass. She had purchased the strongest liquor the store had to offer. Pouring herself a drink, she gulped it down without hesitation. She poured another and another until she could no longer stand without bracing herself against the kitchen's island.

Tears finally streamed down her face; blinding her. She couldn't believe Derrick didn't even mention that his mother saw them. He knew and said nothing. Pouring more alcohol, she took the glass to her sofa, where she curled up into a fetal position. But before downing the last shot, she got up to rummage through her purse for her second purchase that day—a bottle of over the counter sleeping pills.

Flipping the cap from the bottle, she poured half the contents into her mouth. It took several tries to swallow the entire bottle. Sobbing now, she stumbled back to the sofa where she drew herself into the tightest ball she could manage. Her life was ruined because she gave into Derrick. She deserved to die.

***

Janice let out a sigh of relief while she poured herself a well deserved glass of a 2007 Gaja Barbaresc, plucked from a case she insisted her son purchase for her on a whim. She knew she was hard on the girl, but if she couldn't convince her son to stop the madness, she knew Tessa would. The mere thought of her mother finding out was enough to put the fear of God in her. She always suspected the girl was loose, but never to this extent.

Sipping from her glass, Janice congratulated herself on rectifying the wrong without ruffling her son's feathers. He was still her son regardless and she didn't want to upset him. He might get the notion to cut her off and she couldn't have that.

Smiling, she took a healthy gulp of the red wine and moved to her home office to continue with her plans for her trip.

Chapter 42

Cymone eyed Allison while she fussed over Myka. She hadn't forgotten about her betrayal. After Myka's surgery, Allison swept into the room all distraught of her 'friend's' injuries. Cymone wanted to slap her silly.

She, Garrett, Nate and Allison were all gathered in Myka's room. After Myka's cousin KT saw for herself that she was out of danger, she hugged her before leaving her to her friends. Although Nate had called Cymone about Myka, she assumed Allison learned of the incident from news reports, because she certainly hadn't called her nor had KT. And surprisingly enough, Queen was MIA and had been, since the day Myka decided to kick her to the curb. Even so, Cymone fully expected her to show up at the hospital too, but she had yet to appear. She found this strange even for Queen.

The one person nobody expected or wanted to show up was Derrick Steele, who crashed the party twenty minutes after Allison arrived. Cymone wondered if the timing was planned, so as not to draw suspicion that they were sleeping together. She couldn't tell by their behavior. In fact, Cymone thought she caught some tension coming from Allison. Could there be a lover's spat. If so, Derrick didn't show any emotion one way or the other. Allison's behavior could easily be explained by his rapt attention to Myka. Cymone was sure this didn't sit well with her.

And she had to hand it to Garrett, she could see he wanted Derrick out of the room the moment he entered, but he kept his cool while he wished Myka a speedy recovery and then was on his way. Like her, she was sure everyone in the room wondered why he had shown up at all. It wasn't as if any of them were friendly. Myka had made it quite clear that she was done with him. And after she moved on with Garrett, it was more obvious now than ever.

"Is there anything that I can get you or do for you?" This was Allison. She was acting as if Myka had one foot in the grave.

Cymone rolled her eyes. She knew her behavior was due to guilt, nothing more. Nate caught the action and had to suppress a grin behind his hand. He knew Cymone wanted to strangle her. Myka and Garrett were oblivious to the whole situation and Cymone was going to make sure it stayed that way; at least until Myka was out of the hospital and back at home.

Myka chuckled. "No Allison, I'm fine. Stop fussing over me. The doctors say I'll live. She gave Allison a hug to reassure her. Cymone's mouth tightened at this.

Myka was almost giddy. She was feeling no pain from the medication the nurse had given her earlier. She was too relaxed to even worry about who may have done this to her; and for that, Garrett was grateful. He didn't want her to worry about anything other than getting well. He caught Nate's attention and motioned for him to come with him outside.

Stepping into the corridor, Garrett squeezed the back of his neck. "I can't believe they still don't have any information leading to Unger's arrest. Somebody had to see him."

Nate shrugged. "The cops said, even though the sun was out, it was still pretty cold and most folks were wearing hoods and scarves, so no one saw faces that may have been close to Myka when this happened." Myka herself had a cap pulled down around her face along with a scarf.

Garrett was frustrated. Jason Unger had to be the luckiest SOB on the planet. He had managed to kill several people and attempted to kill two more and no one saw a thing. He shook his head at the man's luck. But luck or no luck, he wouldn't stop hunting him until he was behind bars, awaiting a needle to his arm; and this time it wouldn't be an idle threat.

"Man, I gotta hand it to you. You didn't go ballistic when Derrick showed up; not even a sneer." Nate chuckled. Any other time Garrett would have shown him the door in a not to kind manner.

"I must admit, I hadn't expected him, but he and Myka did date, even if it was for a short period of time. At least his gesture showed he isn't completely heartless. Besides, it wouldn't have done any good to get Myka upset. She's my top priority right now." Derrick was the least of his problems. Until they caught Jason Unger, he would not rest.

"Say, what was that with Cymone and Allison?" Garrett detected the sarcasm dripping from Cymone the moment Allison arrived. He thought they all were the best of friends.

Nate half smiled. "Believe me man, you don't even want to know." He would tell Garrett later. But now, it wasn't even worth mentioning. It would just give Garrett one more reason to hate Derrick.

***

Derrick left Metro Regional barely concealing the anger that was just beneath the surface. It took everything inside of him not to smash Garrett Pleasant's face in. It should have been him standing there holding Myka's hand not Garrett.

His anger wasn't because he had any sympathy for Myka. Her getting hurt didn't move him one bit. In fact, he could have cared less. He just wanted to be in the position to savor her pain. He may not have been able to hurt her the way he'd wanted, but to have her laid up after being stabbed was good enough for now.

Chapter 43

Tessa's eyes fluttered open. Her head felt all light and fuzzy, and she had no idea where she was. Fighting to keep her eyes open, she squinted towards the sounds that were coming from a group of machines. It barely registered that she was in a hospital room. Clearing her throat, she slowly turned her head at an intake of breath coming from the other side of the bed. She locked eyes with Cameron who had been worried out of his mind. The tension that had drawn his face, softened when Tessa appeared to recognize him.

"Honey, how do you feel? You gave me quite a scare." He pressed a hand to his chest in dramatic relief.

"What happened?" Try as she might, she couldn't remember a thing.

"You were supposed to have your hair done this afternoon, so when you didn't keep your appointment and weren't at your desk…well, I came looking for you." Tessa never missed an appointment with Cameron without calling.

"And it's a good thing I did too. I found you on your sofa out of it with an empty pill bottle next to you on the floor." He shook his head. "Sweetie, I couldn't wake you so I called 911 and vah-lah; you're now back in the land of the living. Girlfriend, you frightened this old queen nearly to death." Cameron fanned himself with a hand, as if he needed reviving.

When he reached her apartment he knocked and knocked without an answer. When he tried the door, it was unlocked, so he let himself in where he found an unconscious Tessa.

At the mention of the pill bottle, Tessa bolted upright, hyperventilating. It all came rushing back to her; Janice, Derrick, everything. She wished Cameron had let her die.

"Oh god, oh god…Cameron what have you done! You should have let me go!" Tessa was hysterical. Two of the nurses had to come in to calm her down.

Cameron rubbed Tessa's hand after she was sedated. He didn't know exactly what happened to make her want to take her own life, but he would bet it had everything to do with her cousin Derrick Steele.

After learning of the true nature of their relationship, he could certainly see *why* she did it. He was one of the few people who knew the two were related. Tessa had confided that Derrick wanted it that way. Cameron had always assumed it was because Derrick viewed Tessa as beneath him and didn't want people to know he had the likes of her in his family tree. But now he knew better.

"Sweetie, do you want to tell me what happened? You know I would never tell a soul." And he meant it. Contrary to what most people believed, Cameron kept all of his clients' secrets; especially Tessa's, since they were best friends.

Tears welled up in Tessa's eyes, while she told him everything.

Chapter 44

Once she left Myka's room, Allison sighed with relief. She was able to pull off the performance of a lifetime.

Allison's eyes had widened when she caught the news break, that Myka had been rushed to the nearest hospital alive, but in critical condition. The news reporter credited the skills of a local surgeon, who happened to be in the vicinity, with saving her life. Allison couldn't believe it. She grabbed her coat and rushed right over. She had to see Myka for herself.

Once she made her way to Myka's room, she stood just outside the doorway to steady herself. Her nerves were on edge, and she knew she needed all the calm that she could muster before she set foot inside. Not only would Myka's new man, a trained prosecutor who probably scrutinized everyone, be at her side, but Cymone, who could smell deceit ten miles away. She knew she may able to fool Myka, but not Cymone. She didn't want to do or say anything that would give her a reason to look in her direction with too much attention.

When she stepped inside the room, Allison placed all of her focus on her friend. She gave the others a quick and polite nod of hello, before she bee-lined it to Myka's bedside. She said all the right things and gave all the appropriate sentiments and gestures a loving, caring friend should. Feeling no resistance, she was relieved that no one was the wiser to her treachery.

Everything was going well until Derrick arrived; causing her heart to race double time. She couldn't believe her eyes when he waltzed into Myka's room with a huge bouquet of flowers. But what was even more shocking, Garrett let him. This proved that Derrick really wasn't over Myka and that angered her. She was still smarting from their last encounter, when he basically threw her out of his home. She watched him shower Myka with concern while everyone quietly looked on. It made her sick. Once again it was all about Myka.

Although angry and hurt, she did everything in her power to keep a straight face, as not to give herself away. While Derrick did his perfect rendition of a caring, sympathetic friend, she glanced over at Cymone. She could have sworn she knowingly smirked at her. But the expression was there and gone so quickly, she convinced herself she was imagining things. After all, how could she know?

After Derrick left, her heartbeat returned to normal and she was grateful. With him in the room, her composure was just that more difficult to keep intact. And although it wouldn't have been in their best interest to acknowledge her, she was still a little put off that he didn't even glance in her direction. He acted as if they never were together. This alone helped her to regain her focus; that and her need for self preservation.

Before leaving, Allison gave Myka a hug and words of encouragement. She had done her duty as a friend and it was time she left before she slipped up. As she rode the elevator down, a thought occurred to her. Where the hell was Queen? If anyone would have been there posted at Myka's side, it would be the president of Myka's kiss ass fan club. In fact, she hadn't seen or heard from her in weeks, not that it mattered. But it was odd that she wasn't around. And had it not been for her situation with Derrick, she would have made it a point to ask Cymone about her.

Dismissing this, Allison shrugged. She had her own worries. Besides, Queen was a big girl and could take care of herself.

***

Queen watched Allison exit the elevator and push through the lobby doors leading to the parking lot. She still couldn't believe Allison's betrayal. Myka trusted her. The backstabbing tramp couldn't wait to slide between the sheets with Derrick the moment Myka dumped him. She should have known it was more than curiosity involved when Allison became so interested in Myka's love life. Sure she had been interested in their relationship too, but for different reasons. She wanted to protect Myka from the likes of Derrick Steele.

Forgetting Allison and her deception for a moment, Queen wanted to see Myka so bad she could taste it. But she couldn't. Myka didn't want her in her life any more. Besides, even if she were to show up, Cymone would probably have her physically removed by the police. In fact, she was sure of it. The way Cymone felt about her, she may even accuse her of harming Myka, considering the news reports said the police had no leads in the attack.

She had gone up to her floor earlier, hoping no one would be there. But just as she rounded the corner, she saw Cymone enter her former friend's room. So there was no way she could see Myka without a confrontation with Cymone, Myka or both.

Queen sighed. She missed her. She just wished things could have been different. She shouldn't have played Myka so close. But after her own experience with domestic abuse, she didn't know any other way to keep Myka safe. She knew in her heart that Derrick Steele was no good for her. He had all the same traits her former boyfriend possessed. Queen was grateful Myka had seen the light and had gotten out before things turned bad.

She never meant to hurt Myka, just be her friend; her protector. Queen sighed. All of that was over now and she had only herself to blame.

Chapter 45

Derrick frowned when he answered his door to find his mother on the other side. He hadn't heard from her since she walked in on him with Tessa, with the hope that little scene would have rid him of her forever. Now he discovered he was not so lucky.

Without a word, he left the door standing open and strolled back to his great room where he was still stewing over the scene in Myka's hospital room. Not only was Garrett there, but it appeared his old friend Nate had cozied up with her merry band of followers as well. And after observing the unspoken gestures and body language, Nate was sleeping with Cymone. He was very good at reading nonverbal signals and theirs spoke volumes. That skill had helped him more times than not in winning most of his court cases. And Allison. She hovered over Myka like a mother hen, as if *she* had nothing to hide. Everyone he knew and despised had a place in Myka's life but him, and it angered him to no end.

"What do you want mother, or should I even ask?" Derrick gruffly addressed Janice; all the while eyeing her as she made herself comfortable in one of the overpriced chairs she'd personally chosen for him.

He had to admit he was curious, considering how they left things the last time she was there. His foul mood deepened. Janice Steele never ceased to amaze him. She was like a bad dream that kept repeating itself, no matter how hard you tried to wake up and free yourself from it.

"I'm here to discuss my trip to Las Vegas with the girls. It's coming up soon and I need more than my usual allowance to have a good time. We never got around to discussing the particulars."

Janice was as sweet as pie. That whole ugly incident with him and Tessa had long been discarded from her realm of importance. She wasn't about to let anything stand between her and what she wanted, and that included her son sleeping with his cousin.

Derrick shrugged. "If you would've waited until after I finished satisfying myself with Tessa, we could've discussed it then." But you ran out of here as if you were on fire." Derrick gave his mother a sick, twisted grin, while all of the color drained from her face. She never expected him to bring that topic up and he knew it.

Clutching the chair's arms for support, Janice's lips tightened. "Must you be so vulgar?

Derrick raised an impatient brow. "For you mother? Yes!" He was tired of her games and demands. It was high time he put her in her place once and for all.

"You know," he knocked back the drink he was holding before continuing. "You have yourself to thank, for me bedding cousin Tessa, since you insisted she come live here before I had a chance to move in good. Do you want to know how easy it was to get her to spread her legs for me? But then again, I'm sure you remember how persuasive I can be." Derrick grinned at her again.

"It's all your fault you know." Derrick got up to pour himself another drink. "You continued to turn a blind eye to my persuasive skills with those girls back in high school. You knew what I was doing and never said a word. You even defended me when the angry parents showed up at our door. What did you think would happen when I became a man mother? Did you think I would just grow out of it?" He flung his free hand through the air. "Is that what you told yourself?"

Derrick turned to study Janice. "So when Tessa showed up on my doorstep..." He shrugged. "Well, old habits die hard. And did matter that we were related? Not at all. She was just another woman that I had to have." He shrugged again, before raising his glass in a twisted salute before downing the drink.

As tears streamed down Janice's cheeks, Derrick openly scrutinized his cowering mother; thoroughly enjoying her pain. On some level, he always knew he hated her, but it hadn't hit home until now. He hoped she never got the image of him and Tessa in bed together out of her head. He wanted it to be burned into her memory for the rest of her life. He finally realized, the only reason he slept with Tessa was to get back at Janice. Hell, everything low and dirty he had ever done was an act of revenge against her. Janice Steele was every bit of the ball busting bitch his father claimed her to be. She may have broken her husband, but she would never get the opportunity to break him. He would see to it.

With vigor, Derrick launched into his mother with as much ire as he could gather; releasing all the fury and frustration he had tamped down for all those years. By the time he finished berating his mother for everything that was wrong in his and his sister's lives, Janice Steele left his house running again. But this time she was running from the damning truth.

Chapter 46

Cymone felt eyes on her, but couldn't find them in the crowded lobby. Was Unger now after her?

She had raced out to the parking lot, hoping to catch Allison before she left. She wanted the skank to know she was on to her, but Allison had driven off before she could have a word with her on loyalty and friendship; neither of which she suspected Allison knew the meaning of.

It was just as well. What she had to say to her, would have more than likely end in a heated debate that could very well have landed her in jail. And as much as she wanted to beat the crap out of her, she did not want to spend the night behind bars. Although she didn't think Nate would allow her to spend any time in jail, she didn't want to put him in that position. She could just see the headlines now: 'Prominent Attorney's girlfriend lands in jail after beat down'.

Searching again for the source of the uneasy feeling, Cymone shivered. It was time she headed back upstairs before Nate came looking for her. She told him she was just stepping into the hallway to make a call. Had he known she was going after Allison, he would have stopped her or insisted that he join her.

Maneuvering her way through the throng of people, she smiled. The time she and Nate spent together was more than she could have asked for. He was the man she had longed for most of her life. She had to pinch herself sometimes to be assured that it was all real. They may have been thrown together by unfortunate circumstances, but she was enjoying the time with him just the same. After pressing the call button for the elevator, it opened with Nate inside.

"Hey, I thought you'd gotten lost."

Cymone grinned. "I thought I might have a few words with Allison before she left. But lucky for her she was gone by the time I reached the parking lot."

Nate shook his head; pulling her into his arms for a kiss. "When you didn't come right back, I assumed as much. So I thought I would come and rescue you."

"Humph, if I had caught her, *she* would have been the one in need of rescuing."

"Well in that case I'm glad you didn't. But if you had, I would have gladly defended you in court." They both laughed, as they entered the elevator back to Myka's floor.

***

As the elevator doors closed, Jamal stepped from his hiding place. It had been a close call. Just as he was about to turn the corner, Cymone exited the car. He was on the run and the last person he needed to bump into was the person who wanted him in jail the most.

He was there for Tessa. Not having any money to leave town, he had gone to her apartment to see her. He was pretty sure she was the only one in town who didn't know he had been arrested. Tessa never had time for anything as trivial as news broadcasts or newspaper headlines. He was counting on this to sweet talk some money out of her to leave the city, before the cops found him.

But when he arrived at her place she was being loaded into an ambulance. It had taken him a couple of tries to discover which hospital she was taken to. He hoped whatever was wrong wasn't too bad, because he needed that money and needed it now. He had been wondering the streets since his escape; sneaking food and clothes from a shelter, all the while staying clear of the police. But his keeping a low profile was becoming increasingly difficult as more news reports flashed his photo across television and internet screens. He needed to leave Metro City today.

After making sure there wasn't anyone else lurking around who could readily recognize him, Jamal took the stairs up to Tessa's floor.

***

In his assessment of the hospital lobby, Jamal managed to overlook someone who did recognize him— Queen. She was about to leave herself, when she too spotted Cymone getting off the elevator. She had barely dodged Allison, before she attempted to leave again, only to be stopped by her sudden appearance. Unlike Tessa, she had watched the news and knew Jamal was a wanted man. Reaching into her purse for her phone, Queen decided to do a good deed for the day. She made an anonymous 911 call detailing Jamal's whereabouts. Satisfied with this, she left the hospital with a smile.

***

Just as the stairwell door closed, Cameron entered the corridor from Tessa's room. Jamal turned away before he was seen.

"What the hell is going on? Is everyone in Metro City in this hospital today? Jeez." Successfully dodging Cameron, he made his way to Tessa. She was lying in bed with her back to him. Slipping inside, he quietly made his way to her bedside.

"Tessa? Tessa, baby you awake?"

Tessa turned at the sound of Jamal's voice. "Jamal?" She sat up quickly to embrace him. "What are you doing here?" She was glad to see another friendly face, even if he had deserted her.

"I was at your place when they brought you here. Baby I missed you and wanted to see you, but imagine my shock when I arrived and they were loading you into an ambulance. I got here as soon as I could." He held her tight and kissed her.

"Are you alright?" He looked her over for any signs of trauma.

Tessa's smile faltered. She couldn't tell him why she was really there. Telling Cameron had been traumatic enough.

She waved away his concern. "I'm fine. I just passed out, so they just want to run some tests to make sure everything is ok. I just hadn't eaten enough today that's all." She hoped the lie sounded good enough for him not to ask any more questions.

Jamal smiled. If that was the case, maybe he could persuade her to leave with him to the nearest ATM to float him a loan. He was just about to ask her if she felt well enough to leave, when the door opened to several policemen, along with the man he recognized kissing Cymone down stairs. And if that wasn't enough, Cymone was right by his side, arms folded. Jamal's shoulders slumped in defeat.

Queen's tip had been on point. When the police arrived, passing Jamal's photo around, one of the doctor's recognized him entering Tessa's room. Nate had been alerted after the tip and had joined the police in the search. And not to be left out, Cymone insisted on joining them. She wanted Jamal to see her face when they slapped the cuffs on him. She was all smiles when they led him away.

Chapter 47

"Did you ever learn why Tessa was admitted to the hospital?" Garrett was asking Myka. He was helping to settle her into her own bed.

After Dr. Payne deemed her well enough to be discharged, she couldn't get out of the place fast enough. She had spent an entire seven days in that hospital room with her only reprieve being taken to various labs for tests.

Myka shook her head. "No. I tried calling her a couple of times but the phone went straight to voicemail. Mark said she hasn't been back into the office, so I don't know what to think."

It was bad enough discovering Tessa had been admitted and was four floors above hers, but she was more than surprised to learn that Jamal had been arrested in Tessa's room. She, like everyone else, had no idea Tessa even knew Jamal let along dated him. She wondered what else was going on under her nose that she knew nothing about.

"Well, I didn't want to say anything, but you do know the fifteenth floor of Metro Regional is designated for patients with…" Garrett made circular motions with his forefinger aimed at the side of his head.

"Psychological issues?" Myka was shocked.

Garrett nodded. "And since she only spent twenty-four hours there, it's safe to say it was for evaluation. So whatever happened, it was enough for the doctors to keep her over night."

Myka was more than curious now. Aside from her questionable behavior when it came to men, Tessa didn't seem the type to need any mental help.

Pushing that aside for now, she wondered about the other drama that happened that day. "Do you know how Tessa knows Jamal?"

"Apparently, Tessa met Jamal some months back at his former place of employment, a car rental service. They hit it off, and dated until he stole Cymone's money and had to drop out of sight. She claims she didn't know about Jamal and Cymone and I believe her. Why would she know? I'm sure Jamal never discussed his dirty dealings with her.

Garrett kissed Myka after getting her settled. "Anyway, the Jamal case is solved and it's time you get some rest." He wished the Unger case could be solved just as easily.

Chapter 48

Worry covered Mark's face while he waited for Tessa to answer her door. After learning she had been hospitalized and not getting an answer on the phone, he decided to pay her a visit. He cared for Tessa and didn't wish to see any harm come to her. He asked Cameron about her condition, only to hit a wall. He knew the man was protective of her, but he only wanted to help. Mark refocused his attention when he heard the lock release.

"Mark? What are you doing here?" Tessa hugged herself. She had been hiding out in her home since being released from the hospital. She didn't want to go back to the office just yet, if ever. She was afraid everyone would find out why she was there.

"I'm concerned. Can I come in?" Mark had no intentions of leaving until he was satisfied she was well.

Tessa bit her lip. She really wasn't up for company. The only person she let inside was Cameron. He had come by earlier to check on her and bring her food. Resigning, she opened the door wider to allow him entrance.

After she turned from closing the door, Mark immediately noted her paleness and weight loss. Tessa was dressed in ill-fitting sweats and her hair was a mess. It also appeared she had been crying. He had never seen her like this before. Something was terribly wrong and he wanted to get to the bottom of it. He was just about to inquire about her health, when there was another knock at the door. It was Derrick.

Tessa's eyes widened as she silently begged Mark to be quiet. She stood before him with her hands clamped over her mouth while Derrick pounded on the door, demanding to be let in. After a while he gave up and left. It was then, and only then, that she relaxed. Beaconing for him to follow him into her living room, Mark complied.

Thumbing towards the door, he spoke. "You want to tell me what's going on?" he asked; joining her on the sofa. He gathered that Derrick Steele was behind whatever was going on with her. While he waited for an answer, his gaze moved from her face to scan her body for any visible injuries. He was sure Derrick had harmed her in some way. He saw no bruises, visible ones anyway.

Tessa pulled her feet under her before she spoke. "Mark, why are you here, really?" She wondered if he came to genuinely see about her or to belittle her. If it was the latter, he was too late. Her Aunt Janice had already taken care of that. She knew one thing was for sure. Mark wasn't aware of the sorted mess she had gotten herself into or he would be laying into her right now.

Mark cupped her face. "Tessa I care for you. I know it may not have seemed that way, but I do. The things I've said to you over the years…I realized I went about things the wrong way. The things I said were only out of frustration, because I knew you could do better. Baby you sell yourself short. You are a wonderful woman who deserves better than what you've allowed into your life…the men you've allowed into your bed." Mark shook his head. He wanted her to understand what he was feeling for her at that moment.

Tessa stared at Mark in shock. All this time she thought Mark hated her.

Seeing the confusion in her eyes, Mark pressed on. "Tessa I want you to know what good love looks like; tastes like—feels like. I want you to know all those things with me."

Mark had no intentions of spilling his guts when he came to Tessa, but after witnessing her defeated demeanor, and with Derrick pounding on the door, he couldn't help himself. And before he could stop himself, he pulled her into his arms and kissed her.

***

Derrick paced the lobby of Tessa's building. He wanted to know where she was. He tried calling her at her job, but the temp said she was out on sick leave. He called her home and her cell but received no answer. He needed to see her. He needed a warm body to take away the frustrations of losing Myka. Giving up, he was about to leave when Tessa's neighbor across the hall stepped inside.

"Oh, hello. I see you've come to see about Tessa." The older man stated. He had befriended Tessa when she first moved in and often checked on her.

The man didn't wait for an answer before he pressed forward. "It was a shame what happened. The poor girl. I assumed it was man troubles that pushed her to try to take her own life." The elderly gent shook his head. "I was here when the ambulance came. I overheard one of those EMT fellows say she took an entire bottle of some pills."

Suddenly, as an afterthought, he squinted up at Derrick. "I hope you weren't the reason she tried to kill herself young man." He eyed Derrick with suspicious contempt.

Derrick, grateful for the information, assured the old man that he was not the villain. He told him Tessa was his cousin and he was worried about her, since he hadn't heard from her in a while.

Well this opened the man right up. He told him everything he needed to know and hoped he would be around to help her back on her feet.

When Derrick left, his jaw was clenched tight. He may not know exactly what happened, but he was certain his mother was at the root of it. Had she said something to upset Tessa? Was that why she had been so confident in returning to his house the last time demanding money? Making his way to his Lexus, he pulled out his mobile phone to dial his mother.

Before she could finish hello, Derricked demanded, "What did you say to Tessa?"

Chapter 49

Garrett was beyond frustrated. He liked rooming with Myka, but he hoped they caught the son of a bitch Unger soon before he struck again. He couldn't understand it. There was still no word on him; not a sighting, nothing. He never credited the man with being this smart. Most criminals were caught within hours of their crimes. It had been weeks and the police were no closer to finding him. It was if he did his damage and just faded away until the next attack.

Myka was well enough to return to work and against his better judgment, she completed her first day without incident. There weren't any unusual calls or visitors so that was a plus for the day. He hoped it was a good sign that Unger had decided to leave Myka alone. He much preferred he stayed focused on him and not go after those around him. But if the man's pattern held true, Nate was most likely his next target. And with this in mind, he and Cymone had around the clock protection. This made him feel a little better.

Bringing his thoughts back to Myka he watched her as she thumbed through his revised manuscript. With all that had been going on, they still managed to complete it.

She would hand over the task of applying the final touches to the editor in the morning.

He shook his head in wonder. They had completed the final draft of *Criminal Intrigue* before the projected deadline. It was set to hit the stores in less than a month. The book's trailer and advertising campaign were already well on its way, with the publicity showing very favorable in the literary industry. At least he had something to be proud of during this whole mess.

He smiled at the reaction Nate, and some of his other colleagues had, when the existence of the book was made public. Many were surprised to say the least. Apart from his family, no one could have been more proud than Nate. He grinned broadly with congratulations, stating that he knew he could do it. No matter what, he knew he could count on Nate.

But there was one aspect of him becoming a published author that he never expected. The so-called friends who quickly became naysayers. Some even hinted that they didn't think he could pull it off or that he wasn't good enough to be a writer. This part of the process surprised him. People whom he thought would have supported him, turned on him. He shrugged. He would never understand human nature.

It didn't matter. Whatever opposition he faced, after Unger was caught, he would be leaving the district attorney's office. It was time that he moved on; book success or not.

Turning his attention back to Myka. They hadn't made love since she was hurt. But he was about to change that. Walking over to where she sat, he took the manuscript from her hands, pulled her to her feet and lifted her into his arms. It was time they reacquainted themselves with one another.

Chapter 50

Tessa stared at a sleeping Mark. She couldn't believe how he made her feel. He had come to her days ago and never really left. Sure he would leave to go into the office and to pick up some things from his own place, but he always returned at the end of the day.

After he professed his love, she thought he would take her to bed then, but he hadn't. He wanted to wait. Over the past few days, they talked, laughed and got to know each other; really know each other. She learned more about him in two days than she'd known in two years. They actually talked and shared intimate details of their selves. Something she had never done before. No man had ever cared enough to want to know her the way Mark had. And on top of everything that had happened, she felt lucky that this man wanted her in his life.

Things were wonderful between them, but Tessa was growing uneasy with the fact she still hadn't told him why she was taken away to the hospital. That was one fact she wanted to keep to herself, but she knew if she wanted a real chance with Mark she would have to tell him everything. When she finally disclosed her relationship with Derrick, she feared he wouldn't want her anymore.

She felt sick just thinking about it. What had she done? How could she have allowed herself to be caught up in Derrick's web? She knew from the beginning what they were doing was wrong; perverted even.

She remembered the first time she laid with Derrick. She was a guest in his house with little to no money and nowhere else to go. She felt she had no other choice but to give into his demands. Tessa swallowed. How could she have been so stupid? Her aunt was right. This was her fault. All she had to do was say no, even if it meant sleeping on the street.

As if she conjured him up, there was a knock on her door. Tessa glanced at the clock. It was after 2 a.m. Quickly she rose to answer it. She knew it could only be Derrick at that late hour. She looked back at Mark once more before closing the bedroom door. She was grateful he was still asleep. She hurried along to keep Derrick from waking him.

Tessa pulled the door open and stepped into the hallway; effectively blocking the entrance with her body; preventing Derrick from coming inside.

"Derrick, what are you doing here?" she whispered. "It's late!"

The move was not lost on Derrick, but he chose to ignore it. "I talked to my mother, she told me about the conversation the two of you had." Tessa could only frown. She said nothing, while she waited for Derrick to get to the point.

"Tessa…" Derrick tried caressing her cheek with the back of his hand, but she moved away from him.

"Aunt Janice was right. We should never have slept together in the first place; we're first cousins. It was sick! I was sick! Derrick, it's over!" Tessa lowered her voice more. "I shouldn't have ever let you touch me and for that I will have regret for the rest of my life. But like I said, it's over, so please leave me alone!"

"That's not what you were saying when I was giving you the best sex of your life," Derrick sneered. He attempted to cup one of her breasts. Tessa pushed him away.

He laughed. "Tessa, don't fool yourself. You never had a choice in whether or not I touched you, as you put it. If it hadn't happened that night, I would have just waited and worn you down. You know I always get what I want, always. And far as you and I are concerned, it's not over until I say it's over. So whoever it is that you have in your

bed, have your fun tonight, but after that, get rid of him."
And with that he was gone.

Tessa stood in the hallway shaking. What was she
going to do? She couldn't lose Mark. Not now, not after
finding him. He was the only man who ever loved her. But
if she didn't do what Derrick wanted, he would ruin her;
she was sure of it. She had been with him long enough to
know he could hurt her in ways that left no physical scars.
And Derrick's psychological scars were always much
worse.

Tears streamed down Tessa's face, as she let herself
back into her apartment. What was she going to do?

***

While Tessa mulled over her options, Mark made
his way back to bed. He wasn't asleep when Tessa left the
bed. As soon as she cleared the room, he got up to see what
was going on. He stood on the other side of the door
listening and what he heard angered him. He knew Derrick
and Tessa had an odd relationship from what he witnessed
at the office, but this was beyond anything he could ever
have imagined. Derrick had basically forced Tessa, his
cousin, into a sick and twisted excuse for a relationship.

He wanted to kill Derrick Steele. How could one
man be so vile and disgusting? Never in a million years did

he think Tessa and Derrick were related. When he witnessed their behavior at the office, he merely assumed it was Tessa's way of getting back at Myka. Now he knew better.

Pretending to be asleep, he closed his eyes when he heard Tessa enter the room. As she slipped into bed beside him, Mark vowed to free her from Derrick Steele once and for all.

Chapter 51

Mark stood at Derrick's desk staring the man down. He eyed him steadily. He wanted it to be clear that he meant business and was not backing down. Derrick Steele was going to leave Tessa alone.

He assumed there were others who stood in that very spot who had been afraid; he was not one of them. Mark understood the likes of Derrick Steele. He was a bully, plain and simple. And like any bully, he just needed the right person to stand up to him. He was that person.

After leaving Tessa's for work that morning, he decided to take a detour to Derrick's office. He couldn't get back to sleep after learning of his relations to and with Tessa. He wanted the man's head on a platter, but would have to accept the next best thing, a confrontation.

Derrick rocked in his chair amused. So Tessa's little playmate wanted to play guard dog. He was surprised to have the man storm into his office without being announced. He doubted Mark knew who he was dealing with, so he gave the man some leeway before physically removing him from his sight. He couldn't believe he had the balls to stand there and demand anything, let alone for him to leave Tessa alone.

Mark took in Derrick's smug demeanor. He had dismissed him as insignificant before he could finish his sentence. He knew he would have to play hardball to get any results. So if that was what it took to free Tessa from this madman's clutches, then so be it.

On the way to Derrick's office, he had a discussion with Cameron. If anyone knew the full story Cameron did. He had to tell the man he knew of Tessa's secret before he divulged anything. Mark had to hand it to him. Cameron was a true friend when it came to Tessa and he appreciated that. Mark discovered that Derrick was indeed the reason Tessa was hospitalized. Cameron confided that Janice Steele, Tessa's aunt had blamed her for the entire ugly mess. He also learned how Derrick carefully hid the fact that he knew Tessa, let alone was related to her. This was his way of controlling her.

When Cameron found out he was going to confront Derrick, he wanted to come along, but Mark knew it would be better if he did this alone, just in case Derrick decided to be difficult. But he didn't think there would be a problem once he revealed he knew his secret.

Releasing a deep but confident breath, Mark played his hand. "I think you will leave Tessa alone," Mark told him with some smugness of his own.

"Oh yeah and why is that? You're going to make me?" Derrick chuckled. He couldn't believe this guy.

Mark calmly shook his head. "No. But I'm pretty sure you don't want the world to know how you forced your cousin into a sexual relationship with you." That did it. Mark watched the smugness drain from Derrick's face, as he slowly sat forward in his chair. This was the last thing he expected Mark to say.

Although he tried to remain unmoved by this revelation, Derrick's left eye twitched. Aside from his pale exterior, this was the only other indication that Mark had literally hit a nerve.

Mark spread his hands wide in the air in front of him. "I can just see the headlines now, 'Prominent Lawyer Sleeps with First Cousin.' And with all the other scandals this city has seen in the past few months, the media sharks will be in a hysterical frenzy. Anytime a high ranking figure, or in your case a well to do attorney, is involved in a sex scandal as juicy as this one…well, I don't have to tell you what the implications are, do I?"

Hammering his point home, Mark leaned in and pointed a finger at Derrick. "And just in case you missed the gist of this little conversation, let me be blunt. You stay away from Tessa, do you hear me? Or I will make sure everyone in this city knows what a sick bastard you really are." Mark eyed Derrick a final moment before storming out of his office.

Derrick, finally recovering from his shock, was enraged. Some one knew his secret. He wanted to throw something; tear something a part. But he remembered where he was. He was in his office at one of the most prestigious law firms in the country. He couldn't destroy the room without having to answer questions.

It was nine o'clock in the morning but he desperately needed a drink. Stalking over to his full stocked bar, he poured himself a hefty glass of vodka and swallowed it in one gulp. His hands were shaking by the time he returned to his desk.

If Mark knew, who else knew?

Chapter 52

"Hey what's up?" Nate poked his head in Garrett's office. He had asked him to stop by.

"I just had an interesting conversation with Eric Valero at MCPD headquarters."

"Oh yeah, about what?" Nate came fully into the room and took a seat near Garrett's desk.

"You remember how we couldn't figure out how Unger managed to make bail?" Nate nodded. "I guess that bothered Eric more than it did us, because he had one of his investigator buddies do some digging. The money used was routed through several dummy corporations. The more they dug the more complicated it became. This was no amateur. Then there is the fact that no one has seen Unger anywhere, but he still manages to come out of his hole to wreak havoc. And get this. Eric mentioned he spoke with the officer who processed Unger when he was arrested. The man was sure Unger only had a few dollars in a beat up old wallet. But when he was released, the wallet contained several hundred dollars, and there was a brand new cell phone among his belongings that wasn't there when he checked him in."

"Unger has a partner?" Nate's mind was trying to process this. "If he does have a partner, it would explain why the police can't find him. He's probably holed up somewhere in luxury, considering the person who bailed him out has to be swimming in money."

Garrett nodded. "And there's something else. The investigator went back to the last place Unger was seen, the rundown motel. He was able to question one of the residents, who said he saw a man go into Unger's room the night before the police got there."

"Did he get a description?" Nate didn't like what he was thinking and held his breath for the answer.

Garrett nodded again. "The man was tall, white with dirty blond hair, dressed in black. He claimed what made him notice him, was the expensive haircut and the fact the man must have had money, because he was wearing a gold Rolex. And before you ask how a down on his luck bum knows a Rolex, the guy use to drive for our former mayor, who had one exactly like it."

"A Rolex, huh? So this dude does have money." Nate's mind was racing. "But tell me this, why would anyone in their right mind help this scum?"

Garrett sighed. "That's the key to this whole thing. Think about it Nate. The sophisticated set up of the corporations, the money, white male; Rolex…any of this ringing a bell?"

Nate knew where he was going with this but… "Come on Garrett, why would Derrick help Unger? Hell, how does he even know Unger? Man this is crazy!"

"Derrick hates me man—"

"Not enough to aid a killer! Think about what you're saying. Unger killed his family. He tried to kill you *and* Myka. I'm just not seeing it. Derrick couldn't be a part of this. No way!"

But Nate could see it. It was just so unbelievably incredible that Derrick could hate Garrett that much. He couldn't even begin to wrap his mind around this, even though he himself had briefly come to the same conclusion. But Derrick helping Unger? He swiped a hand down his face. This was big.

Garrett pulled a single piece of paper from his desk drawer and handed it to Nate. He knew he was having a hard time accepting it. He even balked at the notion until Eric handed him that piece of paper. It was a composite drawing of the man the witness saw at Unger's motel. It was a drawing of Derrick.

Nate scanned the sheet of paper and closed his eyes. There was no more doubt. "Now what?"

"We wait for Derrick to lead us to Unger and arrest them both."

Chapter 53

Derrick slid under the wheel of the stolen car calmer now than he was earlier that day. Mark Cannon's revelation had shaken him to the core. But once he scrutinized his visit word by word, he concluded that no one else knew about his affair with Tessa. He also came to the conclusion that Mark Cannon wasn't going to tell anyone.

Derrick reasoned that Mark must have overheard his and Tessa's conversation. It was his fault. He was usually so careful about discussing their relationship where anyone could overhear by chance. But he was so focused on keeping Tessa under is thumb, he violated his own rule. Well that could easily be fixed.

After making sure Tessa knew nothing of her boyfriend's knowledge of them or his early morning visit, he decided to take care of him the way he took care of Jason Unger. He would have to kill him too.

Jason Unger had been a tool; a means to an end for Derrick. After overhearing Unger's rant of revenge against Garrett and Nate, he was amused that someone might have ruffled Garrett's feathers. But the humor ended once he realized Garrett was pursuing Myka. He saw Jason Unger as an opportunity to extract his hatred and revenge against Garrett.

After paying Unger's bail, Derrick paid one of his trusted men in the police property room to place the money and cell phone in with Unger's belongings. Unknown to Unger, Derrick had placed a tracking device inside the phone to keep up with his every move. He followed him to the diner and watched him while he eyed Nate. Derrick didn't have a beef with Nate, but if he had gotten in his way, he would have taken care of him too.

He waited a couple of days to see if the man had it in him to find things on his own. But when it seemed he didn't have a clue, Derrick helped him along, by giving him the whereabouts of his wife and son. But little did Unger know, it was a set up. By the time he made it to the scene, Derrick had already torched the house, killing everyone inside. He didn't even flinch when he heard the screams of the dying occupants. It wasn't anything to him. Just like Unger, they were a means to an end.

After he made sure Unger was 'spotted' in Garrett's neighborhood, he followed him back to his motel. Killing him had been easy. The man was a creature of habit if nothing else. Derrick waited in the shadows, while Unger drank himself into a stupor and passed out. Letting himself into the man's shabby motel room, he placed a pillow over his face, thoroughly snuffing out his life. He had served his purpose. Every law enforcement agency in town was looking for him for the murder of his wife and child. He placed his body in the trunk of his 'borrowed' car; drove to the outskirts of town where he had dug a grave earlier that day and buried him. Now it was time to do the same with Mark Cannon.

Derrick followed him from Ellis Publications to his home on the east side of town. Lucky for him, the man had a two car garage and had left the door up, while he went inside to retrieve some personal items before heading back to Tessa's. Derrick boldly backed his car into Mark's garage. Once inside, he tried the door leading from the garage into the house to find it unlocked. He chuckled. People really should lock that door, he thought. Letting himself inside, he followed the sounds of drawers opening and closing.

Moving quietly, he rounded the corner and was on Mark before he knew it. Derrick punched a startled Mark as hard as he could knocking him to the floor. The two men tussled before Derrick wrapped his hands around his neck strangling him. Lifting the man's lifeless body, he hurried out to the garage and placed him in the trunk. Confident in his tasks, he never saw the black sedan pull away from the side of the road to follow.

***

Kobe West followed Derrick deeper into the countryside, taking care that he wasn't seen. He had to thank the short winter days for giving him the anonymity he needed. Kobe had followed Derrick from Ellis Publications to a house known in that part of the area as the country. The homes were spaced apart by acres of land in either direction. He fully expected Derrick to lead him to Unger, but by the time he pulled close enough to the house without being detected, Derrick was exiting the long driveway. Not knowing if Unger was inside the house or not, he decided to call in the police while he continued to tail Derrick.

Kobe had been shadowing Derrick since he discovered his connection to Jason Unger. He and Eric agreed he should be assigned to the detail instead of the police, since they only had the word of a known criminal that Derrick was involved.

Marshall Holmes, the man who claimed to have spotted Derrick visiting Unger, had been Craven Wallace's driver, during the time the former mayor was involved in the criminal activities that landed him in prison. Although

Marshall had been arrested along with Wallace's crew, he turned on his former boss, netting him no jail time for his cooperation.

Another reason Detective Valero wanted Kobe in on the case, was to keep his girlfriend KT Ellis, Myka's cousin, in the dark. If she'd known the history behind Myka and Derrick's relationship, not to mention that he tried to kill her, there wouldn't be anything he could do to stop her from hunting the man down and putting an end to him. It was hard enough keeping her away from the investigation without her learning those facts.

When they came to a wooded stretch along the highway, Derrick turned off onto a gravel road. Kobe killed his headlights and followed; being careful of his surroundings and being careful not to be seen. Once he estimated that he was close enough not to be detected, Kobe left his car; following the road along the tree line, towards the glow of Derrick's headlights.

When he was close enough without being seen, he watched Derrick unlock the trunk. Before Kobe could wonder what was going on, a man popped up from the dark space, striking Derrick. The two men fought while Kobe pulled his gun and ran towards them. They were so intent in pounding each other, they didn't hear him approach. He had to fire a warning shot to get the men's attention. He instructed them both to lie on the ground while he attempted to call for help. But before he could, out of nowhere, police lights and cars swarmed the place.

***

"Man, how did you know I was here?" Kobe asked Eric.

Eric rolled his eyes. "KT placed a tracking device on your car. She was trying to sneak out of my house to follow you, when I caught her. She found out I asked you to dig into Unger's release and decided to keep tabs on you. But when you called in the address to Cannon's house, I made her promise to stay put while I backed you up. I didn't know what you were walking into, so I called out the cavalry and tracked your signal." Eric shrugged.

"I'm glad you did. I had no idea Cannon was even in the trunk until he popped out and decked Steele."

At that moment, the dogs Eric had ordered on the scene went crazy. Both men ran to the spot where several officers stood looking on. Personnel from the crime lab had discovered a body in a shallow grave. By all accounts, it was Jason Unger.

Eric hadn't gotten the entire story from the two men sitting in separate squad cars, but once he saw the freshly dug grave, he could guess the gist of it. From what he could piece together, Derrick Steele had planned to bury Mark Cannon in the empty grave. So it wasn't a stretch to think Derrick had killed Unger, but why? That, along with many other questions, would have to wait until they got back to the station.

Chapter 54

Blake Steele swept into police headquarters with all eyes on her. Tall and beautiful, she drew attention wherever she went and Metro City's main precinct was no different. Even the criminals stopped their pleas of innocence to watch the stylishly dressed woman make her way through the room. She was there to speak with her brother.

Kobe West was coming out of Detective Eric Valero's office when they both noticed the hush that had settled over the open area. Kobe was about to ask what was going on when he caught sight of the woman headed in their direction.

"Which of you is in charge here?" Blake demanded of the two men. She looked from one to the other. After letting her gaze sweep dismissively over Eric, her expressive eyes returned to Kobe. Kobe stared back.

"Miss..." Eric started.

Bringing her gaze back to Eric, she replied, "Steele. Blake Steele. I'm here to see my brother." Blake lifted her chin; sternly glaring at Eric as if he should have known the obvious.

"Well Ms. Steele, I'm Detective Valero and I'm in charge of your brother's case. Won't you step into my office?" Eric gave Kobe the side eye, as he gestured for Blake to precede him. He could tell from her tone that this was not going to be a pleasant visit.

Kobe nodded at them both before excusing himself. With the attitude that woman had, he knew Eric had his hands full and was by no means interested in sticking around for the fireworks.

Not interested in entering the office, Blake turned slightly to watch Kobe exit the station, before turning her attention back to Eric. "Where is my brother?"

***

Blake Steele caught the first flight home after her mother called to inform her that Derrick had been arrested due to a huge misunderstanding. Even though her mother irritated her to no end, she still loved her. She knew Janice Steele was going out of her mind with worry over her precious Derrick being locked up. Blake was under no delusions as to who was her mother's favorite. Janice made that quite clear early on, after Derrick was born.

The eldest with only a year and a half between them, Blake always played second to her dear brother when it came to their mother. And after their father died, Derrick only became more of their mother's golden boy; depending on him for everything. Janice never sought Blake out, unless it was to criticize her for some imagined misstep. She never saw her daughter beyond a pretty face that she had to compete with.

Blake had married young in order to escape her mother's constant drain on her self-worth. The marriage only lasted a few months before her new husband died in a plane crash that netted her millions, by way of the airline's negligence. With her natural skills at playing the stock market, Blake had parlayed the settlement into enough money to take her into several lifetimes. She had hoped, with her wealth and position, as one of the top financial brokers in the country, her mother would have given her some credit. But this seemed to propel Janice into criticizing her more. So having had enough of her mother's wrath and her inescapable devotion to Derrick, Blake resigned her position and left the country. Now she was back.

After cajoling her to join him in his office, Eric pulled out a chair for Blake to be seated. "May I ask why you would like to see your brother? Are you an attorney or is this a family matter?" Eric wanted to know why it was important for her to see Derrick.

Blake let several beats pass before she answered him. "I've been out of the country for a couple of years and I haven't seen him since I left. My mother informed me of the charges and I want to see him face to face to try to understand how all of this came about." She gestured around the room to clarify herself. To Eric, that gesture said, this was all beneath them.

Eric sighed. There was no real reason for keeping her from seeing her brother, so he picked up the phone to call lockup.

***

Derrick sat on a metal chair as he waited for his visitor. He was expecting his mother. She would be the only one who would come to see him. Derrick could just imagine the wheels turning in Janice's head. She was no doubt scheming on how to get her hands on his estate while he was locked up. That would be the only reason she would come to this God forsaken place; the only reason indeed. But to his surprise, his sister stepped through the door.

Blake studied her brother, while the guard perused her shapely legs and backside as she strolled passed him. She hadn't seen Derrick in a few years, but he hadn't changed. Even with all of the evidence stacked against him,

Derrick had the nerve to still have an air of superiority about him. Some things never changed.

Derrick reared back into his chair. Blake was the last person he expected to see. She never cared much for him because of their mother. She blamed him for Janice's behavior of showering him with all of her attention and adoration; leaving Blake to fend for herself. Derrick's lips lifted into a half smile. If she only knew how he envied her, because Janice left her alone to live her life without restraints.

Blake took the chair across from her restrained brother. Derrick had traded in his expensive attire of tailored suits and gold watches for a cheap orange jumpsuit and shackles.

"Derrick, what have you gotten yourself into?" Blake couldn't believe all the charges they were holding him on: murder, suspicion of murder, attempted murder. Her head was still swimming after talking to the detective. Janice had her believing Derrick had a mere misunderstanding with Mark Cannon. Now she'd learned Derrick tried to kill Mark along with a couple of other people. Not to mention accused of being responsible for the death of another man. She knew her brother was a controlling, manipulative ass, but this was a little too deep even for him.

Derrick shrugged. He didn't want to talk about his troubles, because that would mean they were real. Somewhere in his mind he thought he would beat the charges. As far as he was concerned, the police only had a fight between two men, nothing more.

"I think the question is why are *you* here?"

"Mother called, sounding desperate and pitiful. She's concerned about you."

Derrick laughed. "The only thing Janice is concerned about is my money. She's afraid she won't be able to get her hands on any of it, if by some chance they put me away. She called you, because she wants you to bail me out. My funds have been frozen for obvious reasons." Derrick lifted his chained wrists.

Blake sighed. There was always a catch when Janice was involved. She should have known she didn't want her there for support, only money. Had she known the true nature of her call, she never would have come. This was why Janice only gave her vague details concerning Derrick's arrest.

"Well little brother, mother may not get her wish. The D.A. is pushing for you to be held without bail." She studied Derrick while he digested this bit of news. Anger gradually colored his face.

He should have known Garrett would push for this. He wished he had stuck around to make sure he died in that fire. If it hadn't been for those nosey neighbors of his, Garrett would have been history.

"That bastard Pleasant is behind this isn't he!" Derrick ground his teeth with fury.

"Isn't he one of the people you are accused of attempting to murder?" Blake added.

Derrick didn't have to tell her whether or not he was guilty. Even though she may have been surprised at the charges, she wouldn't put it past him. It was just a matter of time before he crossed over to the dark side. Looking back, she felt she should have seen this coming, after the first time Janice allowed him to get away with hurting those girls when he was a teen. She lied for him on too many occasions for him not to feel he was invincible. Especially after he continued to skirt the law, due to his 'boyish behavior' as their mother called it.

Derrick shut down after Blake made her point. As before, he had no intentions of talking about his predicament with her or anyone else outside of his attorney. He had chosen one of the best criminal defense attorneys in his field and the man happened to be a partner at his firm. He just needed to persuade his sister to pay the man's fees until he was free again.

Changing the subject, he asked her for the favor. Against her better judgment, Blake agreed, although she couldn't see him wiggling his way out of this mess this time. There was just too much evidence against him, whether he wanted to admit it or not. But he was her brother in spite of it all.

Chapter 55

Myka sat in Garrett's office horrified. She, Cymone, Nate and Garrett had just learned of the charges brought against Derrick. Eric Valero had come to explain.

"Derrick was the one behind the attempts on mine and Garrett's life?" She still couldn't wrap her mind around it. She knew Derrick was a little put off by their break up, but to resort to murder was unthinkable. What kind of man was Derrick Steele?

After examining Unger's remains, the medical examiner determined he had been dead for weeks. They were appalled to learn the evidence proved Derrick killed Jason Unger's family as well as Unger himself.

Eric explained how and why Derrick bailed him out of jail just to use him as a scapegoat. While everyone thought Jason had killed his family, along with his wife's relatives, it was indeed Derrick's doing in order to frame Unger. Since no one else had a motive, he was free to roam the city undetected as the true culprit behind the killings.

Nate shook his head. "And here I was thinking it had to be a mistake that you suspected he was involved in all of this; and in turn, the man had gone on a killing spree. Could Derrick have that much hate for Garrett? I mean, he's wealthy, young and successful...what more could he have wanted? Doing all of this makes no sense."

Garrett shrugged. "It never made much sense to me either. I've never done anything to the guy. And if truth be told, I should be the one angry with him."

"Garrett, you have one thing Derrick could never have, integrity. You have a solid standing in this city. People look up to you. They respect you. Derrick Steele may have been good at his job, but he has none of those characteristics. The man's a sociopath and has been all of his life. He doesn't know how to obtain anything unless it's through fear and manipulation." Eric had seen men like him before, and sooner or later they all ended up locked away behind bars.

Eric cleared his throat and turned to Myka before he continued. "I've explained why Steele involved Unger in his plot, but I haven't explained why he tried to kill your employee Myka. All eyes were on him once again.

"Mark Cannon accidently learned of Derrick's other dirty little secret."

"You mean to tell us there's more? Wasn't that enough? Geez." Cymone thought they were finished with the Derrick Steele saga.

Eric shook his head. "Did either of you know Derrick and Tessa Andrews are related."

"Related!" Myka was the first to express her surprise at this revelation. The others looked around at each other perplexed. No one suspected this. And when Eric revealed the rest, they were floored.

He nodded. "They're first cousins, two sister's children. But that's not what earned Mark a freshly dug grave. Derrick and Tessa were having an ongoing sexual affair."

"What the hell…" Cymone was appalled, as was the rest of the group.

"This was what Mark discovered after Tessa tried to take her own life." Eric explained Janice Steele's part in pushing Tessa over the edge and how Mark came to discover it all. "Derrick wanted Mark dead to keep his secret buried."

"How did I miss that? How did I not know they were related?" Myka shook her head in wretched wonder. She couldn't wrap her mind around it all.

"Derrick went to great lengths to make sure no one knew they were related. I mean, wouldn't you, if you were sleeping with one of your relatives?" Eric asked.

"Derrick Steele is sicker than any of us could have known," Garrett said. "I wonder if he will try to use this as a defense. I can just see his attorney now; pleading him out as not guilty on the grounds that he is mentally ill."

"He would have to be to sleep with his own cousin," Cymone pointed out.

Nate shook his head. "The man is evil not ill. This is just the kind of mind Derrick Steele has and there is nothing sick about it. He planned and calculated every move he made, and the only reason he got caught was because of Mark Cannon. If it hadn't been for Mark, he could have gone on and eliminated all of us and the police would have still blamed Unger."

"Mark is lucky to be alive. Derrick could have killed him instead of choking him unconscious," Garrett added.

Eric nodded in agreement.

Chapter 56

Two days later

Nate closed his fingers around the wound that was now spewing blood. He'd been shot. He peered around the desk for the shooter who was still searching for them in the darkened suite of offices.

"Are you—,"

Nate clapped his hand over Myka's mouth. He didn't want the woman to hear her.

Nate was about to get into his car parked across from Myka's building, when he noticed Allison standing outside looking up at the floors above. He wouldn't have thought twice about it if the woman hadn't looked so disturbed. Feeling the pull to check things out, he made his way across the street. But by the time he'd weaved through traffic, she had already entered the building. Foregoing the elevator he took the stairs two at a time to Myka's floor, hoping against hope that what he was feeling was a false alarm.

Once he reached Ellis's offices he rushed through the glass doors to find the place dimly lit. He called out for Myka, who responded, but sounded frightened. Nate patted his holster to reassure himself that his gun was still there.

Even after Derrick had been arrested and the threat was gone, he still couldn't bring himself to part with it. Moving towards the darkened hallway, he told Myka to stay put; he was coming to her. He found her in the small kitchenette, the only brightly lit room on the entire floor, and she wasn't alone. Allison was there with a gun of her own.

When Nate came into view, Allison trained her focus on Nate. "What are you doing here?" She was irritated that someone else had invited themselves to this party.

"I came to see Myka." Nate studied the woman. He noticed she seemed out of sorts, as if she was not in her right mind.

Angry, she brought her gaze back to a shaken Myka whom she had pinned against the refrigerator. Allison rolled her eyes. "So you've added another one to your collection of men I see. It's bad enough you seduced one man in this office, but here is another one. And I bet he's here for the same treatment.

Allison had come to visit Myka the night she and Garrett made love in the conference room. After witnessing the two go at each other, she was angry because Derrick still wanted Myka, even though she was with another man. That night Allison made a decision. It was time for Myka to relinquish her hold on Derrick, even if it meant she had to get rid of her to accomplish it.

"Why is it that you feel the need to have all of these men at your beck and call, huh? I mean, I don't get it. I'm just as pretty as you…hell more so, but you are the one *they* want." She nodded her head in Nate's direction.

Myka was speechless. She had no clue Allison felt this way. She was closing things down for the night when she turned to find her standing in the doorway. She continued on with her chore, chatting away at her friend; never noticing she wasn't participating in the conversation, until Allison cut in; asking her to persuade Garrett to let Derrick make bail. Myka was taken aback by her request. She was curious to know why she cared if Derrick made bail or not. When Myka refused, Allison pulled the gun from her coat pocket.

Allison spouted on and on about Derrick; reiterating how Myka was messing up her opportunity to make him happy. She blamed her for Derrick's inability to make bond, by refusing to grant her simple request.

Myka tried to explain to her that she couldn't do that, because Derrick had tried to kill her and Garrett. Derrick was where he belonged, behind bars. This had only agitated Allison more. And to Myka's horror, Allison admitted she was the one who stabbed her on the street that day, not Derrick.

Allison had just arrived at Myka's building when she exited to pick up lunch. Allison followed her. When Myka made her way back towards her office, Allison took this opportunity to attack her. Making sure her face was covered, she moved along with the crowd and swiftly stabbed her twice, before continuing on her way. She was sure she had put an end to her rival until she caught the breaking news story on television. But now she needed Myka's cooperation to free Derrick. He was counting on her.

Allison had gone to see Derrick after his bond hearing. Under the circumstances, she didn't think she had a choice. There wasn't any way around it if she wanted to keep herself out of jail. She knew he had figured out she was the one who attacked Myka, the moment the charges had been read in court. Derrick had turned to stare at her. He had guessed her duplicity.

Although Derrick hadn't disputed his involvement in the attack against Myka—yet, she hoped he would keep his mouth shut. It shouldn't matter if he pleaded guilty to the attack on Myka or not. With all the evidence that was stacked against him, he would be going away for a very long time, so why would one more charge matter? She hoped he would agree and not turn on her.

She may have tried to kill Myka and she may have still held a grudge against her, but she had come to her senses. She didn't need anyone finding out she was the one who attacked her so- called friend. And after Derrick was arrested, she had planned to rejoin her old friends as if nothing ever happened. No one would be the wiser that she and Derrick ever had a fling.

But Derrick had a proposition for her. If she could talk Myka into persuading her boyfriend to let him out on bail, he would keep her secret *and* they would go away together. Allison's heart perked up at that. That was all she ever wanted was to be with Derrick.

Allison's gaze swung from Nate back to Myka. She should have guessed the uppity bitch wouldn't go along with it. And now, on top of everything else, another man was involved.

Nate took a step to move further into the room, only to be stopped by Allison's gun, which she now trained on him.

"Don't come in here! This doesn't concern you. I want this heffa to agree to get Derrick out of jail, and then I can have a man of my own. The man who should have chosen me in the first place."

Just as Allison turned back towards Myka, Nate flipped the light switch off, instructing Myka to run. But before Nate could take his own advice, Allison fired in his direction, clipping him in the arm. He felt Myka brush passed him and followed. They ran down the corridor to the conference room where they hid behind a podium. They listened while Allison raged at losing them in the dark. She was heading up the opposite end of the hallway.

"Is there a phone in here?" he whispered to Myka. Nate realized his was in his briefcase which he placed in the car before following Allison.

Myka shook her head before realizing he could see her. "No, the closest one is in Mark's office a little further down the hallway," she whispered.

"We need to move and get to that room to call for help." Nate removed his coat and jacket with some effort. Taking his time, he removed his handgun from its holster. Allison had shot him in his dominate arm. If he had to use his weapon, he would have fire it with his left hand.

"Let's go now and stay close to me."

They made their way to the hallway and down to Mark's office, but before he could ease the door close, they heard Allison rushing towards them.

Moving quickly, they hid behind Marks desk, where Nate winced when he bumped his bad arm against the desk's corner. He had to stop Myka from speaking when he heard the door open. They both held their breaths as they waited.

"Myka? Are you still here?" This was another voice. One Myka recognized as Queen's. Myka almost groaned. What was she doing here? She hadn't heard from her in weeks and she shows up now?

"Myka? It's Queen. Gurl, do you know your front door is unlocked? It's after hours and anyone could just walk on in."

Hiding her handgun behind her back, Allison flipped on a switch that illuminated the hallway. "Queen, what are you doing here?"

"I'm here being a friend which I can't say the same 'bout you." Queen had placed her hands on her ample hips while she glared at Allison.

"What are you talking about?"

"I'm talking about you, Miss Thang," Queen sing-sang, with a swerve of her neck. "I saw you hugged all up with Derrick Steele. What's up with that? You 'posed to be Myka's friend and you screwing her man?"

Queen was also in court during Derrick's hearing and noticed how Allison sat and drooled over the man. Even though she was still upset over how things ended with Myka, Allison's actions had irritated her more. So as her last act of friendship, she decided to let Myka in on Allison's betrayal.

Allison raised the hand with the gun and leveled it at Queen. "The word is 'supposed' you stupid, ghetto bitch. Learn some English." Allison was more disturbed than ever.

While Queen and Allison squared off in the hallway, Myka raised up enough to search the desk for the phone. She pulled it towards her by the cord and grabbed it down to where they were hiding. She dialed 911, while the two women argued. Nate was busy trying to stop the blood flow with his belt he had placed above the wound.

"I might be ghetto, but I am not a backstabbing hoe, hoe!" Queen, not backing down, threw off her coat and kicked out of her heels as Allison charged her. The two women fought and scuffled until a gunshot rang out. This seemed to bring Allison to sanity.

When she let go of Queen, she noticed blood on her blouse. It wasn't hers; it was Queen's. She had shot her in the abdomen.

Allison was horrified at what she had done. She tried comforting her, but Queen pushed her away, before dropping to the floor, writhing in pain. Still angry, Queen cursed at her. A bewildered Allison shrank away from the words as if she had struck her.

Allison back pedaled away from the horrible scene, bumping into a wall, where she stood cowering. Wide-eyed, she flinched at the sound of the police filling the hallway; ordering her to drop the gun.

She quickly dropped it to the floor with a thud, while Queen continued to moan in pain on the floor. One of the police officers moved forward to handcuff Allison, while another knelt to tend to Queen. The officer stayed with her until the paramedics arrived. In the meantime, Myka and Nate had come out of hiding to get Nate some much needed medical attention.

As Nate and Queen were loaded into ambulances, Garrett was rushing up the sidewalk to a trembling Myka.

"Are you okay?" He looked her over before he pulled her into a bear hug. When she called to tell him what happened, he couldn't get there fast enough.

Myka nodded. "I think we should go to the hospital to be with Nate and Queen. I told Cymone to meets us there."

Thankful she wasn't hurt, Garrett took Myka by the hand as they walked to his car.

Epilogue

"*Criminal Intrigue* is number one on the New York Times bestseller's list! We did it!"

Myka shouted, as Garrett swung her around the room. He placed her on her feet just as Nate popped the cork on the first bottle of champagne. Cymone held the crystal flutes for him to fill.

"Man, congratulations! I must say I knew you had it in you. After I read the first paragraph I was hooked." Nate was proud of his best friend. After all they had been through, they deserved some good news.

Garrett took a sip from the glass Myka handed to him, grinning all the while. "I have to thank this woman right here for pushing me in the right direction." He kissed Myka's cheek.

"Gurl—I mean girl, I am so proud of you!" This was Queen. After risking her life for her, not only did Myka see her friend in a new light, but so did Cymone. She conceded that any woman who would take a bullet for a friend was alright with her.

Cymone shook her head. "No Queen. We are proud of *you*; especially me." Cymone hugged Queen, who cried. She had become her new best friend.

After witnessing the love between Cymone and Queen, Tessa fanned her face, trying not to cry herself. After everything that happened with Derrick, their relationship was uncovered. But instead of treating her like a pariah, as she feared, Myka drew her closer; viewing her as just another one of Derrick Steele's victims. Tessa was horrified after she discovered Mark had overheard their conversation that night. But once she learned he didn't blame her either, she let her guard down and they became closer.

Mark pulled Tessa into his arms, kissing her. "When did you become so sentimental?"

"It's just that so much as happened and everyone has been so nice…" Tessa did cry, but the tears were happy tears.

"Well girlfriend. You don't have a thing to worry about anymore. That disgusting Derrick is behind bars for good. So you have nothing more to be anxious about." Cameron took a long sip of his champagne. He was more than happy to see the two of them together. And since Tessa had been with Mark, her entire life had changed for the better.

"What's going to happen to Allison?" Queen asked Nate. She felt a little guilty where Allison was concerned.

If she had gotten past her hurt feelings and come to Myka sooner, maybe she wouldn't have stabbed Myka or shot her or Nate.

"She'll do a few years and maybe some of them in a mental institution. I'll do my best with her." Nate had taken on Allison's case even though she shot him. He felt she too was a casualty of Derrick Steele's mania. Although most of the people in the room disagreed, especially Cymone and Queen, he took the case anyway with Cymone's blessings.

"Well enough of the gloom and doom. We are here to celebrate Garrett's success." Myka raised her glass. Here's to the man of the hour; author of Ellis Publications' first number one bestseller, Garrett Pleasant."

***

Blake Steele sat at the bar, twirling her glass of white wine. It had been a long day. Her brother had been sentenced that morning to prison for the rest of his life, and she had shipped her mother off on a month long excursion through Europe. And to top it all off, she learned Derrick had been sleeping with Tessa. She didn't know whether to laugh or cry.

"May I join you?"

Blake turned her head and locked eyes with the man who sat down beside her. She recognized him from the police station the day she visited Derrick.

Without taking his eyes from her, Kobe raised his hand to get the bartender's attention.

The End

From the Author:

I have thoroughly enjoyed bringing you the story of Myka and her friends. When I began this book, I didn't know if I wanted to continue the Stone Family and Friends saga, or start a new journey. But as I thought about my characters and the roles they were to play, I realized they needed to stand on their own; and maybe, just maybe, began a brand new saga. We will just have to see how that concept plays out.

I hope you have enjoyed *Penciled In* as much as I have enjoyed writing it.

Katrina

Connect with me on Facebook:
https://www.facebook.com/Touchofamansheart